QUERENCIA

SPRING 2025

Querencia Press – Chicago II

QUERENCIA PRESS
© Copyright 2025

All Rights Reserved

ISBN

978 1 963943 44 3

www.querenciapress.com

First Published in 2025

**Querencia Press, LLC
Chicago IL**

Printed & Bound in the United States of America

CONTENTS

POETRY

in the pre-dawn or when
the horizon swallows the sun &
all your pretenses are
an affront
the magma's volatile buoyancy
holds its breath & the shards you show
the blinking void around you
drift into quiet contiguity
core to poles a spine of light

—ANASTASIA WALKER (she/her)

IN ANOTHER LIFE

in another life we just stop by
and you serve us lemonade in mugs

in another life you live alone
and you're dancing around the kitchen
sun spilling onto your counter
singing that your
girls are hereeeeee

it smells like summer
and you
have your gold back

—STACEY MANOS (she/her/ella)

LOQUATS WITH SOLAR ECLIPSE
4/8/24

On the beaches of Mazatlán, the people experience totality
first on this continent. I am in San Gabriel, holding
a metal colander up to the sun.

Mini crescent moons smile up from concrete. In the yard,
I sit in the shade of a loquat tree. Its yellow berries
drag branches low enough for magic

shadows. A play of light and dark with a beginning,
middle, and end. Picking a berry from the tree
and eating its tart meat is a climax.

How I love the taste of its juice on my tongue. I lick my lips
and kiss my fingertips. The eight of cups shows a man
walking away, his back to the crescent sky.

"Walk away from what's abandoned you." I learn the word,
limerence, a state of infatuation with another person
to the point of obsession.

It's a balance of hope and despair. Hope they will reciprocate.
Despair when they don't. Shine and shadow. I knew
I was addicted to the pain of it.

Today, I walk with my back to the diminishing sun and hold
a bowl of little cups overflowing in shadow. Toss
the cups. Watch them multiply.

—XOCHITL-JULISA BERMEJO (she/her)

SUBURBAN APARTMENT

I've burnt myself out writing eulogies to no one,
mourning a past, pinned against the
broken edge of miscarried future—
places you cannot ever return to, even when they live
inside you, always.

Those absent mornings, every watery dawn that pressed itself
against the slits of the venetian blinds,
relentlessly trickling through at the edges.
How each subtle, shifting thread of daylight nudged
the dreamless pillows where we lay,
separate in shared silence. Only the voice under my skin, calling—

> *Show me a world, and I will show you its*
> *grave, each exit wound torn from the same conduit*
> *heart we call home.*

(catching your scent years away
on a nameless stranger, I ask:
is there no heavier burden than
honesty to yourself?)

And still, the return of summer, with its sweet
fruit, reminds me that sometimes a pit can be
stone solid, can be hard as
life.

The pin we orbit is the olive trees—
the oldest in the world. Gethsemane stands,
and we know its name because we
feed it.

History lives only in the space between
tongue and teeth;

I stand and starve with my mouth full of
your name,
twenty-five years
too late.

The crush is inevitable, the shuffle of seasons,
little eddies of time flowing into
one another. Never gone, only
changed.

No matter what shape it resolves itself,
I will give myself over—
learn again to savor that bitter flesh,
to keep the solemn core of regret pressed in my cheek,
where its poison is safe,
its threat far from my throat.

(careful, careful,
don't you see?
This too is a place
where life can begin)

—Sylvia Godreaux (they/them)

TEXAS WAR SHIP

Joshie believes in a place
that isn't here. Texas,
he says, will save him.
I don't call it an obsession
(save that word for myself),
but with shower water prayer
beads on his shoulders,
to the chipped grail sink,
over and over it is muttered:
Texas, save me. Texas,
save me. His faith
is in somewhere else,
someplace better. He
accepts the promise
of endless desert and crude oil.
Of everything bigger.
Yes, there is a lot to deny here—
Joshie, who has not stood
in one place long enough
to walk away, whose pale knees
have not yet been scraped up.
But when I move to say something,
in the space between my buzzing
mouth and open throat,
I am halted. I have no notes.
Really, the truth of the matter
is simple—I will follow him.
Joshie can show me how different lakes
hold their water and how to create
darkness with a slung arm. He can deny
me, and I will take it like a door
to the head. He can think only
in the short term. It doesn't matter.
I believe in the places we can go
together. Joshie can deny me
and I will put my hands
in the tawny vintage—

the spilling scarves, and fresh
rusted spoons—and I will find
another way to be. I will be denied,
I will be denied, I will
be denied. And still, under my breath,
I will correct him gently, *Texas,*
save us. Texas, save us.

—EAMON DUNN (he/him)

BE CAREFUL WITH YOURSELF
—after Julia Jacklin

The coast resembles more
a jawline each day. Too sharp,

it wants for much, I think,
misses the predictable

violences. Hours inland,
my (con)temporary home

holds a faint tidal rhythm. I play
percussion against the walls,

lose the beat quickly. Distance
imposes its limits on synchronicity.

Time an unkind relative,
a begrudging out-of-stepparent.

I don't trust my mind to dwell
here responsibly. I hire

hecklers to tell me the good news.
I take notes, read up. If nothing else,

my solace is well-researched. I've found,
for example, that suddenly shifTING TO

CAPS LOCK IS LIKELY to coax the poet
to smile to themself. Call it soliloquized

science. Grant it equal standing with
the fantasies of ▮▮▮▮▮▮ that soak

my shins in brine and silt. What washes off
easily gives credit where credit is taboo.

Tonight, we're imbibing on azure in the key
of G. My name is on the list, and they wrap

my wrist with a green fabric band. The sun
is a match head in the sky. Rainbows

marble the ground. A professional
drummer accompanies the singer,

and my finger tapping becomes
inconsequential. I decide

there is no lost time, only moments
we're no longer bearing. The wind

is dying down; the hour
is nigh for the flyer to land

her sea cucumber kite. The water
is retreating with all the momentum

of bad stagefright. I slip from the crowd
and walk to the break, convinced

I obey gravity by choice. The rocks slosh
with ripples, suggestions from the fount.

It's just a draining bathtub's gurgle,
a breath that bows the surface.

—ALIX PERRY (they/them)
Previously published in Tomatoes Beverly (Querencia Press, 2025)

ONCE IN BARCELONA

I take the
thoughts
I think them
we wish
once in Barcelona
we shall all sing
without hate
Everything will
be pleasant
and
the revolver
was
the trigger
He
stopped the bullet.
like a sparrow.
Looking at it
black like a crow
beside me
I believe him.

—SARAH KLEIN (they/them)

your voice shyly breaks apart into brass tones, wrecked beyond limitations and friable tissue. its nature is jadegreen sheets of ice and spackled when beyond limitations for mutually assured construction. your body is tesseracted by yards of wreckage for

being a bridegroom when you're just a boy with a bandsaw against the sun, the electric eye beam as an insomnia beat, how it casts out of you, revealing the white textured walls of your lungs when you speak.

it's no accident, but not worth looking over your shoulder for. get patched up with caffeine and try again later, then you can resume driving in the vacuum of space, with deer flying overhead. congrats on the license!

—**tommy wyatt** (he/they)

IS THERE A MALT SHOP IN OCHELATA?

I wish we had been kids
Is there a malt shop in Ochelata?
I wish we had been kids
You'd take my hand
To chirp me, tiny me,
too tiny me,
onto metallic red leather
One barium milkshake—one straw
One soda from the spinal tap—one straw
(That was your growth, not mine)
(I didn't do bubbles)
(I ordered a Hi-C orange)
I would lean my big hair to your big head
And we would wait for my drink to come.

M.A.S.H. list on green construction paper
Facedown in your Mead marbled,
scratched with spaceships
We'll both rent, who cares, but what I'd say as I slipped it to your desk:
You will, tall, towering, show me the photos
Two more than your best friend has even seen
Of years where that head of yours was in proportion
To a begutted body
And I would cross my legs—on your inflexible monk's couch
And I would cross my heart—with the hand holding your 4x6 shame:
I'd want you anyway.

That was me, too, Dylan,
who swallowed the world faminously when returned
One corner piece missing from the biopsy (it's not in the rug, it's not in
the vacuum)
Who felt far too hollow in the whirring tunnel (how can we be so
transparent)
Who fasted for the bloodwork (what could a postmortem Salt ne ever
heal)
With all our shelves had been through
We deserved to swallow the world
One plate—two forks

One bowl—two spoons
You would lean your big head to my big hair,
And we'd wait for our fullness to come.

If I could fly back,
Once more, to that prison mattress couch,
To your sparrow shoulders,
With my rounded arms
I would fix this first before fuckall else:

I would not want you anyway,
I would want you because.

—TARA GIANCASPRO (she/her)

We are a difficult folk—southern sun, northern moon. You became
a hand knocking to solicit any answer & it was only polite for me to hold
my tongue. Mama said *if you can't say nothing nice*—& so I didn't say
anything at all. I became a long exhale of smoke, I painted the walls

yellow & waited for our bones to stop growing. & time answered all
of my questions, all of your questions, time made us understand
that they were the same. Your hands & my fist & every other
coiled strand of us stained with story, with tales of bushwackers

& a righteous revolution, & all our father's blood that spilled
into the earth. Time tore at your body until you became
as small as our mother, bent with the years that would
eventually press her dear heart into the earth & you

would go too & soon enough it'll be me, hobbled
by the pace that I would never let slow. Tell me why
we never talked before you felt the dirt against
your cheek? A fond goodbye follows

a lifetime of silence, & why is this the life
we chose to live? You'll ask mama
when you get there, I suppose,
& I will see you soon enough.

The years apart have grown
shorter & shorter & I will
see you soon enough.

—LE FRANCIS (she/her)

THE CAVE

When I was a little girl, my mother took me by the hand and led me into the wilderness. I must have been delighted by the glinting sun through the dry grasses, the swaying of red paintbrush, the yellow flowers of chamisa stinging a bare sky. The scuttling insects, red mounds of ants, their pleasure lashing my flesh.

I tell it that I was delighted—not because I remember all this, but because that is my ideal of girlhood. One of delight.

After a time, my mother pronounced, "you have your father's eyes," and a trail appeared. But because my eyes had been claimed, I disavowed vision.

We walked a little further together. I heard the sound of the winds through the pine boughs and knew we were gaining altitude. I wanted to turn back, but she insisted. "You never listen," she said, "just like your father." And because my listening had been claimed, I disavowed hearing.

And yet there were the scents of the earth. And because my nose recognized them neither as sources of delight nor disgust, to my mother, they appeared to be of little consequence. These remained, among the senses, unperturbed.

After a long while, we came to stand still. She commanded me to hold out my hands to catch the air. And because my hands—though opened— remained empty, she let me go.

I must have landed somewhere, or perhaps it was that I never leapt.

When at last I opened my eyes, the landscape was changed. What had been dry had become saturated with water. What had been bathed in light, now I knew only as darkness.

In my palms I beheld whorls of green. Mammalian hearts collapsing into caverns. And when I tilted my head, golden liquid splashed from my ear onto the page. In the resulting stains, I discerned forms curving towards me—bell husk, or virgin knife.

In another version of this account, it is the father who leads me there. The outcome doesn't change.

—SONYA WOHLETZ (she/her)

Hopeless Incantation

Only rage was plucked from my hair. Only bitterness, so savage it lit up
the room—all my filth nestled as vulture in my chest. Anger will do no
good here. I repeat: I will not let my mother down, I'll let no one down, no
grandmother, no brother, no sister, no grandfather, no one dead or alive,
consume white smoke, spit out that goo.

Do you promise me another burning day?

Another warming. Another warning of what comes.

Salt the room, salt the circle become the room, the room is the salt after
the fire, the fire is in your heart and the room and in the air.
I do not know the future

but I come screaming at it with open arms.

I swallow.

—Mateo Perez Lara (they/them)

what was she thinking when she died like that?

was she mad at me for not answering her last ever call?
what a horrific way to die, spewing out chunks
of blood-red matter, bloodied mattress
the look on Darias
when I told him *don't go in alone*
the fact he keeps the pictures on his phone, just like our cousin said
the fact is he doesn't grieve
I'm fine
well, I am too, brother of my mother's organs
(now spewed, now dust)
but I'm trying not to numb it out for once
I wonder why
that was the last night
& how that last week
we both didn't sleep
over & over
(called her over
plucked the cyst from her back
put on her dressing
fed her)
dawn breaks
& I am a broken savior
a forgotten one who no one understands
not even Brianna
a piece of scrap metal
turns up on that floor
the blood became it
it shattered, like it really mattered
because she never mattered
how brutal how awful
they all say
& I'm here clinging
but I still wonder
over & over
what was she thinking when she died like that?
how many people did she kill
with all that blood
the way it spilled

the way it piled
the way Teddy cleaned it & gracefully
so gracious
I should be so gracious
but I can't help thinking
about that blood
about those drugs
about the things I haven't said
I need to talk it all out
I can't, I can't
the way Teddy cleaned it up
I slip
I slip & fall
the way I instructed my family to step over
my mother's entire being
pooled into bloodied mess
the way they looked at me
I'm sorry, I'm sorry
well, I'm fine, I swear
it doesn't really matter
it was just a fever dream
she's still here

—JESS TOWER (she/they)

A Train Through the South

Clatter-click, the wheels hum hymnals,
iron devotions through swamp-threaded veins.
Out the window—a preacher,
part-wolf, part-telephone,
howls his sermon into a crescent moon,
dangling low, like an earring, in the ear
of a woman with magnolia hands.
Her fingers glisten, dripping sap or sweat,
a wave, or is it the branches—
bone-white, clawing, waving back?

Cypress trees stagger backward—
bayou soldiers wade into the black ooze,
their boots whispering secrets to the mud.
Hats tilt in slow salute,
silent tongues murmuring:
"Not yet, not yet, your time sleeps still."
A burst of cicadas—machines, surely,
spitting binary in the sultry haze,
and the train lunges forward,
its wheels chewing through memory,
spitting it out as steam.

The windows fog, and I see sepia:
a woman cradles a baby of marigolds;
the petals wilt with every breath.
A man tips his hat to a shadow,
then folds himself into it,
his edges blurring like ink spilled on paper.
The conductor's voice crackles through static:
"Next stop: cotton, next stop: ghosts."

Past fields that ripple with laughter,
the earth grinning where the plow has bitten.
Out here, a horse gallops backward—
no, not a horse, a clock,
its hooves marking time on endless tracks,

tick-tocking into a vortex of kudzu.
The vine creeps, swallowing all but the train,
which becomes a ship now, slicing waves of moonlight—
a schooner, no—a memory,
tasting of salt and a mother's hum.

A child outside, barefoot,
plays hopscotch with gravestones.
The numbers flicker faintly:
1863, 1929, today.
Someone taps the window from the other side—
a finger, not human,
a root grown curious, its bark cracked with age.
It beckons, it pleads,
and the cypress soldiers bow in unison.

The absurd crumbles, flakes away.
The train grinds into its final station—
a street, present and pulsing,
where a man sells honey
in jars that mirror his eyes.
Magnolia perfume drifts on the air.
The preacher's howl fades into a hum
lodged deep in my chest,
and the moon—brass and glowing—
pins itself to my lapel.

—GRADY VANWRIGHT (he/him)

I Place the Cast Iron in the Arms of the Sun

Lilacs linger / in perspiring purple palms / there / my life line / sparkles sweaty / my love line / rings off the hook / my head line / brashly buzzes / a sex crazed bumble / searching for / too bright blooms / love can be / a fortifying & catalyzing force / if you let it / let me / engage with my ugliest impulses / & survival mechanisms / in a different way / a tiny turtle / survived / today / a tiny human / made sure / they could choose / between shore & swamp water / I am choosing / to say thank you / as many times a day / as I hear / birds beckon brazenly / across the park / thank you / sun warmed wood / thank you / friendship frolicking / thank you / countless cats kissing / our ankles & noses / my nose stays red / all summer long / while my freckles fling / themselves / across the banks / of my shoulder blades / one day / I balanced my breasts / as close as they would lay / against / my chest / they met them there / with their generous gaze / I have never felt more / bright / than when / I'm in their direct love light / I will treat / every day with them / like the first lick of an ice cream cone / after a long bike ride / I love sloppy / I love satisfied / I love somehow / more / everyday / today / my neck strains / scanning the ground / for goodies / even I need a break / from the sun / sometimes / I promise / to look up more / morels taste best / bathed in duck fat / on a deck / dense with worms wriggling / their way into / my heart / I promise / to always make room / there's no scarcity / here / in this place / finally choosing / to love me back

—KD Hack (they/he)

COALESCENCE

Your hands spin velvet on my skin.
We are draped in it now,
the tiny hairs that rise in prayer
at the crest of the hip bone,
the howl of something sacred
dying on an ancient hill.
There's nothing left
but the curve you've made of me,
the dark scent of mud, thick and damp.
The swollen earth of you
calls me home.
I want to remember this—
the softness of it,
the clinging,
like moss, memory of the forest.
I want to commit to ritual
the way we hunger in the wet fog,
and all the while,
the needy moon above,
with its big gray eyes, its cavern mouth
asking if we could ever accept
          a half-eaten heart.

—ALINA KALONTAROV (she/her)
First published in Sand Hills Literary Magazine

WHEN WE WERE 16 SWIMMING AT THE LAKE AND YOU SAID I HELD ON TO YOU TOO TIGHT

I am Charybdis,
the monster most avoided,
the most destructive path.
I only whirlpool to gather you nearer,
to feel your presence,
to feel you,
to feel.

I am a lonely beast
swallowing men and ships
and hopes and dreams
to gather a little of their light
inside my own dark belly.
You could pick men from my teeth
but that's only because
I can't hold them against my chest,
I can't hold them,
I can't hold,
I can't.

—CHARLES K. CARTER (they/he)
First published in The Poet Heroic

DAHLIA

another month falls brittle,
dissolving before we can think
of what to call it.
it sinks us under the surface of
encroaching early darkness,
the warning of gentle winter, and how
she will soon come to set it all
back to rights.

i remember it abstracted,
latent as it was, when we lay
on the shore of september's long
shadow, skimming hands and hair across the surface,
so our ears rang with its ancient,
full-bodied sound.

all those days in god's periphery, when the balmy,
fleeting summer air remembered itself by our names,
and i stretched to match your synthetic breath in
awkward, faithless symmetry.

my heart keeps the rhythm even now,
standing outside the house that is not
your home, my eyes instinctually scanning
each window for faint and familiar light.

suburban rows of barren trees raise their supplicant
branches to beg mercy of a shrouded
autumnal sky, obfuscated
with the acrid, heavy scent of brushfire.
the smoke sours the air, plum dark and
mottled as a fresh bruise,
richer than pomegranate flesh.

the earth grows heavy on the exhale
as it remembers how to breathe.
there's so much beauty in an end,

in the arduous necessity of a controlled burn—
how it consumes everything it touches in a bright, sudden
instant, even when your nails splinter with the
anguish of holding on.

slipping into another crepuscular season,
there is only that creeping, soft otherness
where the cold has stolen everything
but sleep. i dream again that you are
leading me to the water,
where we sink to our knees in the mud
of the shoreline, bloated and distorted
by the late-season rain.

we must wait here, wait until
our saturated clothes become too heavy
for second thoughts, until the rushing dark
unfurls itself to fit the velvet
impression of another innocent, sacrificial year.

there are many ways to die
and there are many ways to be
haunted. the leaves that we see
are never the same as the ones
we remember, but in the saffron-tinted
sunlight of another shambling october,
i sit with my temple to the cool glass
of the passenger side window,
and everything rearranges itself into
the long ride home from
school.

—SYLVIA GODREAUX (they/them)

the most wanted person (please please please please please)

think it's cute when girls just want to be wanted. think it's even cuter when America wants her. wants her so fucking bad actually. wants her locked up for life. but to be wanted she has to kill. to be wanted she has to eat. tasty, tasty desire. cannibalism as a metaphor for true love. remember to savor it. for the past week I've been thinking about blood and guts and other lovely things, thinking about all the horrible things I could do. would America want me if I tore off my skin in the shower and ate the scraps. would America want me so fucking bad actually. would America want me locked up for life. sometimes I want. sometimes I want to be. sometimes I want to be wanted. sometimes I want to be wanted the most.

—ERICA LESLIE WEIDNER (she/they)

FOR A LADY

Don't go to the lighthouse
They say it drives men mad
The isolation
No one to hear them speak
Except imagined mermaids
Beckoning on the jagged rocky shards
The only women that'll listen to them
It'll drive you crazy
No one will believe you
When you tell them what you saw
How you felt
Because they know
Its reputation
Don't go to the lighthouse

You bought it, you say
With your own money
I thought you were just a thrill-seeker
We have those, you know
Make their way across the choppy waves
Break into the darkened pillar
But I hear they either don't come back
Or their minds are broken
All of them men
Can you imagine
Being so full of promise
And for that to change overnight
Oh, but imagine, if a man did go
And came back just fine
How proud he would be
How brave
No, no, I'd never go myself
I'm happy right here
I've got a wife
I've got this bar
I've got my job
I'm very important here
But you bought it, you say

What good would a place like that do
For a lady like yourself
Are you sure you know
What you're getting yourself into
Aside from the fact
That it's cursed
It hasn't been maintained in years
I can only imagine
The kind of rot it must have
The kind that sinks into the bones
Of a place, you know
Practically impossible to repair
And honestly, it's a bit of an eyesore
You sure you want your name
On a place like that
Some moldy, haunted, money pit
I mean really
What good would a place like that do
For a lady like yourself

You want to make it into a retreat for women, you say
Retreating from what
A place like that is no place
For ladies
Didn't you hear what I said about the men
Who've been there
Who lived and died there
Good, young, smart men
With their lives ahead of them
Why once I heard about a young fella
Wanted to be a lawyer
But up and decided one day
That he'd rather be a lighthouse keeper
He didn't last one summer, you know
Before they found him dead on the rocks
If he couldn't make it, well
I don't see how a place like that
Could be "uplifting" and "inspiring"

For a lovely young lady
You seem happy
Your face is pretty enough
What do you have to complain about
Honestly, what a joke
Retreating from what

I'll be praying for you
Because you'll certainly need it
Don't you walk away from me, young lady
I am talking to you
See this is what I mean
They can't even handle
A little advice, some criticism
No way they could survive the lighthouse
Did you see her skirt
Just barely covering her ass
That shirt
So tight
Just begging you to look
I mean
What do they expect
When they dress like that
I'd never let my daughter leave the house
If she dressed that way
Those shoes
I bet you she can't run in those
But she's not the type to be running
If you know what I mean
How's a cow like that
Supposed to walk up and down
All the rickety stairs at the lighthouse
She's going to fail, you know
This business she was talking about
Retreat for women nonsense
Look there she goes to pay her tab
Might as well light that money on fire
She hasn't the sense to use it right

Those nails are painted all pretty
Probably gets them done all the time
I bet on her husband's dime
The poor bastard
If she even has one
What a damn waste
I know she sees me waving at her
I know you see me
What are your ears broken or something
I know you can hear me
Turn around goddamnit
Don't you walk away from me
You're going to fail
You're going to die
I'll be praying for you

—MEGAN MCCORMACK (she/her)

"FEMALES"

reproductive woman   stripped
of personhood   christened
scaffolding around womb

her body claimed laboratory
with no name lay an egg for us
females   cluck cluck

send your mother's day card
to the battery farm   females
we've a cage for you   right here

go on   clean the lions' den   feed
yourselves to the keepers   all
the world is a zoo   locked in

females   life seized in the lungs
ventilators birthing the next litter
of wombs   lay an egg for us

females   cluck cluck

—HOLLY ARCHIBALD (she/her)

THE GRAVEDIGGER'S ARITHMETIC

In the beginning, I knew nothing:
Then came subtraction,
the family integer minus one
equaling an unnatural fraction.

And minus one and two and four,
genocide's obliteration is asymptotic.
One body, and one body, and one body
became then eight, then sixteen, then a village.

Mourning is geometric progression.
Nothing common in this ratio,
the calculus of corpse-makers:
demagogues divide, invoking imaginary numbers.

Coruscated parabolas rebuff integration.
Incendiary arcs whine and whistle,
foundations shake and fracture,
shaken by wrathful throbs of a sinusoidal pulse.

In enmity's ouroboros
we can afford no tangents.
And in the bitter smoke, we are inaudible:
amplitude, frequency, these we don't possess.

And in the papers, black and white,
we are reduced to two dimensions,
to brown knobs on an abacus—
the variables of collateral damage.

—MUKUND GNANADESIKAN (he/him)

all the cool kids worship headlines

it is imperative to gaslight yourself. well, you'll get there. but first, turn the tv on.
commiserating coyly with the news cycle will only lead to despair. but it's sexy,
ain't it? it's got a little twang to it.
hoovering has never been so fun and flirty! nothing can compare to the sucking
up of joy leaving your heart clean and pure, ready for the virulent, vile Word;
only what's needed is left.
the three imperative rules of engagement: idealize, devalue, discard (your fellow
humans).

the media seductively begs to neg us into hysteric climaxing. let it guide your
hand down,...down, a little further.
right.
there.
to the part of you that is ready to tap into reveling in the bystander effect. your
mind fizzles, the cotton feeling between your ears a wet fever dream of
divisiveness and calculating hate. it feels like a must, a have to. the tv said so, so
we all must despise each other. order received.

but no. we've been down this path before. our anxious attachment doesn't mesh
well with the crisp avoidant attachment of the system. reject the future faking
and general faking and making faking and revel in community. the resistance and
rising fire fist of joy, warm embraces, and creative, feisty spirit. commune with
moon, with sun. consider yourself a revolutionary whence you look upon your
fellow people with a heart full of beating blood, clear sight, and resolute, gentle
wisdom.
and radicalize,
now.

PS. in the general words of Kendrick: turn the tv off, turn the tv off.

—Rainier McCall (he/they)

A Girl at a Bar is a Call

Slip past the hand, rising,
avoid   the night out at the bar,
smile, less, much less,
     ignore the thing in you that fawns
for the swoosh & strobe of lights against
crushes of bodies.
Avoid yourself entirely,   shadows,
     some with secreted intentions.
You like the acidic rip of close danger,
     the spray of its flesh   mist,
A crowd feels safe. All those hearts.
     Slip past the man,
the one with the Invisalign smile—
     ignore the admiring thought: he cares for his teeth.
Solitude also feels safe. The absences of those hands.
Nurture boredom, think of the weight of bees,
The individual   and the mass,
The buzz of their collected lives.
They swarm when one of their own dies,
Rage unified, small, & yet, a threat   collectively,
To be so united—you'd never die unmourned.
     Ignore the voice reaching out—
Stop punishing yourself with others' bodies   imagine
     If they knew?
     Imagine.
Smile less   much less.

—MADARI PENDAS (she/her)

Eve on Lilith

I still smell her wrists
blessed with blossoms of the apricot tree
drunk on its temptation

find strands of her red hair
streaming like Tigris
in the folds of our bed

hear the animals
exchange rumors with one another
wondering where she has gone

almost feel her gaze
soft, watchful, garden green
simmering like the sun

see the embers
of the fire she lit to cook him a meal
before she was thrown out.

I can only imagine his face
when he found her on a bed of moss
under the curious moon

her hands slippery
and swift as the Euphrates
between her thighs

mouth open, breathing greedily
finishing loudly only after
he ordered her to stop.

—Kali Joy Cramer (he/she)

Fable

—with lines from Mary Oliver's "Wild Geese"'

For our second night together
he gave me a tail
soft and animal
I refuse
to wear it, so it rots
in his dresser, wrapped in plastic
like a corpse in a crime show

Show me what it looks like on
He pouts and rolls me on my stomach
folds me over his knees
his very own roadkill

What can I kill
to make this work?

The hard animal of my body?
Or the soft?
Mary, is that what boys want?
The soft animal is a kink
a privilege,
a fairy tale soft boys whisper
to one another in locker rooms,
under covers, to the mirror
to scare off the big bad wolf

Must I repent on my knees, tail wagging
for the hard animal that kills
because it needs to eat?
I wanted wings!
A harsh call and feathers
Forget the tail! I want the sky
A crepuscular fable that ends like this:

Even with her tail tucked into grandma's
lace panties, the big bad wolf's teeth
could bite a head off, clean

—TOMA ZBRIZHER (she/her)

WHAT IF THIS SOFT BODY IS PREY?
—after Mary Oliver's "Wild Geese"

You catch my scream,
your fingers caressing
my esophagus;
they come away bloody.
Is that not your tender point?
                    you croon.
The soft body of this animal
                    craves
the clutches of sharp teeth.
I spent months circling
my enclosure, snapping
at every passerby, then
wondering why no one
released me. You lurked
just out of my jaw's reach,
                    whispering
*don't bite the hand wound
around your survival.*
The soft body of this animal
thirsts for retribution; apologies
aren't enough, I want to eat
your innards raw. The vultures
will be here soon, regardless.

—MAGGIE BOWYER (they/them)

THE BOD

I forced my orgasm through a straw.
Gelatinous bend, and stretch, and
forgotten on the other side. He didn't
need the Bod. Funnel gathered dust
instead of melted ice cream. Hosiery
gathered dust too. Ripped by grieving
hands. Cocaine of a stranger. Beloved
earring—no more in the plural. I
discovered Bod accidentally. It was
very much scratching. Sixth grade bio
textbook a wet lexicon. Now we
hardly bark at the same car-doors.
Laser face. The Bod speaks for
herself mostly. Panties shrink in
the wash. Poetry al fresco barely
remembered. Boys clamoring
for the clam, forever etched. The
scars are just a checklist. She
is still at the end of the driveway.
Blooded beak flight. I am asphalt
gliding. Looking down through the
whole town. Waiting for someone
to shovel me into the pail. The news
found avian flu in the cow-milk. Mixed
batches of missed opportunity. They
forced their orgasm through a straw.
Talking, decapitated, but budgeted
for full Bod. I subvert the teachings
in my childhood bedroom. I flash-
backward to California. He didn't
need the Bod. Every rose asked
for a picture. Apple owns more of me
than I do. I am learning how to
speak my language in a cold box.
Keating Avenue stayed cold. Hospital
pews were fuller than anticipated.
Two minutes of dick. Post-nasal

highway...ladder... funnel. The
temperature of my skin is a
parabola. My pet snake and I are
learning to adjust. I have a meat
thermometer for just this occasion.
The goop in his sink was blacker
than the tar-eye-bags. Poppers
are skyscrapers descending.
Meth is skyscrapers descending.
The Rock made a movie about this.
My skin has been so fertile. Raise
crops, terraced paddies, reaping
spoiled spoils. Doctors should take my
instruction.
VIVISECT. Ingrates are ringing bells
in the street. Dystopia won. Again. I
wrote a poem about cum so many
times. I'm a genius. Future excuses
injected. Not vaccinated. Heating
the organs to at least 160 degrees.
I flash backward to California. He
talked about marriage. I controlled
myself so well. Held back my Bod, so
well. And the Bod held me back too. I
forced my orgasm through a straw.
And I could no longer see what was on
the other side.

—ELLE JAY SNYDER (she/her)

The Ruins

Watching over you
in room 4060
on curve 25.
Let's get some air.
Primal cries set against
a backdrop of
sea lavender and purple roses.
Standing by your side in
midnight gardens
at the grave.
I got to hold you
in your pain.
Baby, keep your head up.
I'm reaching for your hand,
until the end.

—Kimberly Madura (she/her)

BLOOD-RED SHEETS

Stay in bed with me, under these blood-red sheets. I forgot
how you taste. Can you remind me? It's nine forty-eight and
we can stop time, if we try. Your hands on my back, your legs
holding my legs. You make me laugh and shudder and sigh.
Let's annihilate the past and the future, too. We've no use for
what's in their maws, dripping with contempt and gore. I only
want to be here with you. Please, please stay. I don't trust
that things will turn out well, so I won't let them turn out
at all. Hit the pause button on the remote for me, okay?

—PRIYA SAXENA (she/her)

PEDESTRIAN STRUCK

I couldn't sleep when I cut me.
People would look past the blackened walls,
maybe resolve two impossible things.
I could be shiny.
And I would be gone.
When I performed
my double talk
fire shot out the chimney
and no one saw the knife.
I couldn't sleep when I cut me.
I could make you God;
unattainable, and always disappointed.
A face unremembered
in two headlights.
Touches displaced.
But I couldn't rest until
I saw the indents
scabbed over. The beeping louder
than the multilingual screaming.

—ELLE JAY SNYDER (she/her)

He Dissolves Me

Stage 1: tissue rot with gold fillings, drips softly from where he touches,
silver down an inverted spine, my skin retracts to reveal that I did not
issue a quiet forgiveness, my predator will go out screaming.
*

Stage 2: Heavy, his burden when he leaves me at the bottom of the
trench just beside the train. My belly full of his misgivings. Flies incubate
terrible secrets, now I'm holding on to them, wait until I burst.
*

Stage 3: with my body-paste, I write my name in the dirt. I name each
maggot poking through. My grave-wax reminder of more carnivorous
times. He will remember.
*

Stage 4: diagenesis, bone remembers its duty, its punishment, its lasting
guilt, a shame that echoes. How do you sit with yourself at night? Do you
pray? Do you peel back your own scared skin, I am coming, let me in.

—Mateo Perez Lara (they/them)

Bones shaping her flesh,
the mare stands at my man's
left side. He does not know
I am barren, and I have not
found the words to tell him
there will be no sons with his face,
no daughters to protect from
the attentions of boisterous boys
with more desire than sense.
The mare prances through furrows
made by cold metal plows,
nuzzles the hand of the man
I have given my years.
When I call his name from
the porch, she neighs, buffs
his arm with her hide. When
he reaches for me, the mare
discovers green summers,
joins the herd and mates.

—COLLEEN S. HARRIS (she/her)

TRIPLE DOG DARE
        —*after Lucy Dacus*

Crossing Butte and 2nd on Saturday
        afternoon, you'll come upon our
finger painted miniatures: not the stuff
        of fantasy games, but cheese boards
and house cats and two-pack toothpaste.
        The domestic necessities, according
to us. Besides practiced dexterity,
        our secret is using an extra-long
pinky nail for the final refinement.
        We sell our work with complimentary
shots of green tea. There are days
        when we are tempted to open a café.
There are days when we ruin the brew
        and offer it with many words of caution.
Our regulars mind their manners and
        shrink their sips. Depending on the
season, the chill of the evening or
        the swarming of its bugs chases us
back to the truck. The windows stay
        rolled down even in winter because
the hand cranks are broken. Repair
        would bring new comforts and ruin
old ones. We bundle up and blast
        the heat while yelling out what we
want for dinner. Our dishes are
        nonsensical inventions meant
to trick the ears: ginger ale
        seashell salad, grilled monsteroni
and cream, tomatoes beverly.

We compare notes in the driveway
and explain our fantastical dishes
        as if they are well-known delicacies.
And so on we will continue until
        the engine gives out and we sell
the truck for scrap like we've agreed
        and we get rides from friends
whose car windows keep us warm.

—**ALIX PERRY** (they/them)
Previously published in Tomatoes Beverly (Querencia Press, 2025)

صبار prickly pear cactus: a marker of bulldozed palestinian villages

flowers open-mouthed
like ripened citrus,
it's pulp and fruit a marvel
of cool sweetness,

after its spiny hairs are plucked
and thick waxy skin is sliced
in   halves,
its carved belly trickles
stored rainwater,
like sloshing tears,

there are clustered patches
standing like faces
everywhere,
climbing up, gulping dry air,

their roots damp, thriving,
soil soaked
with martyrs' sweat,

immovable.

—JAWEERYA MOHAMMAD (she/her)
First published in Berkeley Poetry Review

OBSERVATIONS ON COLLECTIVE SELF-OCCULTATION

Trapped between faith's boulder
and a cracked cement foundation,
in a moment of annularity,
we risk eclipse
under acrid showers of white phosphorus
and whine of rockets whistling overhead.

Let oval rings of fire delineate
a common boundary.
Circumferential joining.
Walk the perimeter, hand in steady hand.
Clear the air of cacophonous cries,
let symphonies of thrush and wren return.

—MUKUND GNANADESIKAN (he/him)

On Duplicity

maybe we get it from our fathers
who treated every boundary

like a line drawn in quicksand
always so skilled

in straddling the limit
growing roots on either side

or maybe from our mothers
who thatched the roofs of their inner lives

shelters clayed in stolen time
where they birthed themselves in secret

perhaps it's the puma on the prowl
who has taught us

to never walk fully exposed
in the light of day

that to drag home the spoils of conquest
one must first reconcile with the urge to kill

or maybe it's the gazelle
who leaves us her inheritance

she knows to keep her shadow close
that to survive is to split in two

so that the hunter
can only ever find

the weaker one of you

—ALINA KALONTAROV (she/her)
First published in Sky Island Journal

FORCED TO WATCH

My body changes How it looks—
Whether or not—it's being watched
A littler and bendier body in the eyes of a lover
depending on the lighting
I'm Much less intimidating
In the day time when the only shadows are under my eyes
In between my legs
or In the folds of my sheets

A less daunting form when in flux
When in nosedive
Much gentler after a 3 day bender
Skin feels so much softer—in the blackness of one's room
Even more so in someone else's

I could use someone else's
In someone else's room
I'd alter my values for it
I'll morph to it
Pay for it
Might end up Praying to it
Be polyamorous for it

I'd like to think I could be different
look, a little different
Change parts of myself
Only, small parts of myself
Like the size of my upper lip—
The thought of it
Makes me keep a mustache on
Cause the one time I shaved it off
Later that day, while riding my bike, I got hit by a car
and the lady who hit me, jumped out asking if I was okay,
Stopping mid-sentence
to say
Instead
" what are you? "

I pretend she was curious about my species
And not my gender
I try to hold sliding doors for myself when I arrive unannounced
at the end of the date
I don't want to have had to use my head at all
My feet ain't budged a bit

I want to go to places I love by myself
entering rooms in the same revolving door section as them
Not moving an inch
Let those pretty fingers float right above your knees
Right below my skirt
Let those delicate wrists lift only what they neeed to lift
Only what they want to
Like finger tips that pry my eyelids open
When I've fallen asleep too soon for you to see how I get when I'm alone
Ask me to be more
When you haven't had your fill of me

Let them forearms with those tiny tattoos not stress a vein
Keep them bones calm inside my skin
Let me do all the work
Plant your foot down
Dig your heeels in
elbows softer than bed sheets
Soft as they are coerced to be
They WEREN'T put there by god to shoulder for room
Or to shimmy a way through
But to stand crooked fists on hip bones unmoving for anything

—ETHAN VIETS VANLEAR (he/him)

WILL YOU REMEMBER MY NAME?[1] —tommy wyatt (he/they)

how long will i feel anger as a somatic response to
you breaking up with me at the psych ward, you
said, "i wanted to be sure you're somewhere safe, i
hate to do this over the phone," soon the line clicks, you did
not consider how my memory shifted to a wormhole,
collapsible from its structures, since i surrender

truth formed by others who have operative conditions to steer your
love all the way to the left when the only way out is through. what life
have we lost if its existence is a hypothetical structure that goes
for a stretch of time, traveling on
with astral fugue, where the wraith of you presses on without
me.

---

[1] A golden shovel of "You Will Remember" by Ember McLain in *Danny Phantom*:
"Fanning the Flames"

DUPLEX AGAINST MEDICAL ASSISTANCE IN DYING
—after Jericho Brown

State-sanctioned death is not the solution
I ask the State: what problem is solved by death?

I demand, *what problem is solved by death?*
Tired of thinking death can solve my problems.

My problems with life made death delicious:
Suicide is born in the need to escape.

The need to escape births suicide,
What if you had a life you could live in?

What if you had a life you could thrive in?
What if prolificacy affirmed your life?

A resourced existence is life-affirming,
Our lives are curtailed by scarcity.

Manufactured scarcity destroys life,
State-sanctioned death is not the solution.

—TIEZST "TIE" TAYLOR (they/them)

do not go gently you whose bones shrivel and warp, you whose guts churn and perforate, you who are missing your flesh, your organs, your mind: you who know the shuffling away, the categorization, the minimization, the torture, you who have suffered under the clinical gaze, the familial gaze, the white gaze, the male gaze, you who have been ignored, you who have had everything taken away

rage, rage against the taking of your life

—SARAH KLEIN (they/them)
Previously published in Maddening Mast Cell Mathematics (Querencia Press, 2025)

the clock morphs—
its hands tangled like serpents,
I see it. Eyes falter; they are green now,
rolling down the stairs like marbles—
the stairs I have never known.

The nurses circle in bird masks,
fanning feathers against the cold,
blinking in slow rhythm. "They are nothing—"
I know it—
"more than pigeons," I say, then forget again.

At the window, there's that horse—
brass mane, buckling hooves on asphalt,
pulling a chariot of broken lights—
"Ah, but the war's been done," I murmur,
though the horns still blare.
They should be simple taxis.

In the mirror, a stranger with a hollow face
mumbles about markets—copper, salt,
the weight of words—but he
falters at the syllables.

I nod along as he speaks of coins
that melt between fingers—
a bank of bees, buzzing,
honey sinking into my skin,
but it sticks, it stings.
I know the hive's not real.

I fold the sky between my hands,
tucking the edges like a blanket,
but the clouds—
they twist into soldiers, into lions.
There's laughter. "It's absurd," I think,
the king of rain sits on a wicker throne,
a crown of thistles turning to fire.

His voice crackles like old vinyl,
"None of this, none of it, is true."
I want to agree,
but there's the clock again, slithering.

—GRADY VANWRIGHT (he/him)

THE TAKING OF

Glass was left in the food dish, clue number one.
Maybe all our throats should've ripped open.
Less time wasted on shared, familial trauma.
Forgetting humanity, diagnosis be-damned,
is still always shocking. She asked me the same
questions over and over. I fed her the same
answers. Grandma still only cared about
sustaining her young—whatever vessels
they had now poured into; the many shapes
of inherited love.

I didn't intend to follow suit, to enable
the machinations of a long goodbye. To forget
to eat. Wasting starts in the gut. Says hello
to the spine. Finds its way to the fingertips.
Eyes never settle on their target. I left glass
everywhere. Shared, familial trauma. Forgetting
humanity, never understanding that included
vessels still waiting to be filled.

The looks of disappointment
never seemed to exorcise this forgetting.
We've been running dress rehearsals
of my wasting for a very long time.

—ELLE JAY SNYDER (she/her)

Earnest
                —after Vievee Francis

my mother's husband earns his death each time he crosses the threshold
of my panty drawer
            —steal my allowance money
wanna see a magic trick? beneath my father's abuse
these flesh wounds grow rigid and become my new skin.
paternity confirmed by disappearing singles   and violence
he replicates my mother's name to pass bad checks,
turns her party into blood bath—tile thick with blued crimson,
her limp wrist & lip-biting puddles mapping a path from bedroom
to front door where ambulance belts *this is the end of her.*

loose change throwing doubt at the sturdiness of cardboard,
for Halloween I collect donations for U ——.
dad thickens his pockets with charity
and my school is never the wiser as I am absent so often—
he gets away with chitlins stinking up the kitchen, be it countless injuries,
a fortnight in jail
so many missing pills my mother buys a safe
but by morning he is flipping pancakes in her apron, picking me up from
the schoolbus where the others think I'm tasteless for saying *fuck* and *bitch.*
you curse like a sailor! I want to utter that I don't come from respectable people.
___sponsors us for Christmas, and we move to a house along a different bus
route with a mudroom and a basement.
I learn to be silent on the journey while my foster sister fistfights boys. then my
step father is caught on tape violating the register at work.
just when I think his lies will not feed us, he buys a candy apple two-door.
finally, we have a car!

when it is gone I overhear on the phone that police have recovered the stolen
goods in our driveway, a white van hot to the touch from sun rays houses
rottweilers barking something vicious, and I am only seven,
but I know it is for street fighting;

I suspect the money is good.

we are good again, no more rotten fruit on top of the white refrigerator.
we can afford Japanese candy from urban convenience stores. that January
I have a roaring birthday party with gift cards and extended family.
                    we make a way.

—TIEZST "TIE" TAYLOR (they/them)

As children, my brother and I

kissed the cold earth
and brushed our teeth with
fistfuls of dirt and concrete
to forget the saccharine sweetness of
their indulgence

as the snow sweltered, my brother and I
plowed through old gravel
and dined on frostbites
to hide the grime left in
their journey

as our sun paled, my brother and I
played, forgoing faint breaths
and wished until sparks
blooming like mold sighed out
their pity

as we held hands, my brother and I
smudged colors of winter
and waited for voices to come

to take

to mar

to abolish
our kingdom

with

their reality.

—JIHO LEE (she/her)

THE CALL

Does it come as words
or come from where the words arise,
some threshold in the self,
as far back as you can go in the self
before the candle goes out
and you're left in the dark?

If not as words then as the pigeon calls,
low and distant, far above your head,
invisible on a rooftop this still city noon,
but calling, informing, making a frame
around the picture.

The call is integrated with the quality of the light,
its grammar is the grammar of the weather.
Muted and declarative, the call frames the day,
puts distance in the neighborhood,
points you somewhere new.

—BENJAMIN GOLUBOFF (he/him)

something about low blood sugar and a misogynist playing a
triggering song

When I send off towards the side of your ear an earnest,
is that what you've brought? and you position yourself to better
figure out your answer, I don't come and say, *hi, are you
okay?* so you do the *come* part while I still don't say it—

just look towards you with my ghost-girl eyes,
but you don't talk past the side of my chin.
When I don't offer, *I finished the drink I was guzzling,*
you don't do whatever you never do,

but hahaha, this is not a sad poem, because when I don't resort
to pressing thanks into your arm as I walk away and turn
down my face, I also don't say, *I appreciate you,* so when
you don't ask, *why?* I don't respond, *I don't always know*

*the particular reason. That's why I always tilt my head
at you—I want to know what it is I'm appreciating.* But
I don't mention that, because you never ask, which
of course could be because it's as obvious a thing as I am.

—LYDIA RAE BUSH (she/her)

Between lay-about leaves we cling
with brittle feeling sing like the gales
between the hills. Haunt the corners

of the sky, red ink blotted, crystal summer
sea breaks the horizon, waves lap
the shrouded boards, last painted

in '92. I run a finger through
the elements of yesterday's
ghosts, the last breath

of the Tyee fire lingers
in my lungs. Yet all which
once was, now has scattered—

like bones, like words, like myth. Again,
I strain to hear your voice above
the clearing of my throat, a season

in between. I itch & think of you
like a fire that could clear out
the underbrush. Good god,

don't you ever doubt how I would
love you if you would just let me.
Constant as this cough, with my

heart-red eyes. Sure enough,
I will suffer for this world
& that is how I know I am alive.

—LE FRANCIS (she/her)

PRACTICUM FOR GENTLENESS

Hello, my darling! Come. Sit in this tub
I call my heart, so that I can wash your hair.

Dip your head back. Don't worry. I won't
let soap sting your eyes. See how

I pour the water warm and away
from your face? Feel it run over shoulders.

I promise, you can relax. And after
I'll towel-dry your curls. No rubbing, ringing,

or roaring of a dryer. No rush. Instead, I'll hug
each bead from your precious head.

Trust me. I know your fear of knots.
And when it's time to brush hair,

I'll begin with the tips making my way up.
You won't even know where hands work.

No screams. No tears. You'll be so confused,
you might need to laugh. Let out what must.

Finally, I'll weave long tresses into two loose braids.
No yanking. No pulling. Two ropes made of you.

—XOCHITL-JULISA BERMEJO (she/her)

WEIGHTLESS IN THE SURF

I see it stretched before me
nestled in the vulping trees
Slopping land warping as my mind slides
Over
Grasping at an image
I can solidify
Into reality
The burning of this body
The gnaw unwavering in the bones
The overripe organs
Swollen, threatening to rupture

Spill out
Onto this mattress
Fill the imprints left by bodies laying
Day after day
Year after year
As the foam rolls
The dust and grey flecked debris settling
Between the framed lathes
And holes burrowing up
Clawed out nests
In the box spring
Wheezing coils under the weight

The grating hum blaring (deafening thrum)
Of blood down blocked (ear) canals

Flowing
Liquid
Imagine

From this bed
This death bed
This coffin I slide into
The pain
Grousing
Lunging

Dreaming
Between nightmares.
The fractured pace of dreams
Flashing between waking moments
Like my heartbeat faltering with my breath
My pulse as if a switch
Turning me on and off into
Blackness, nothing
On the intense light—white
The rolling of my veins
The tiny vessels
Creatures teeming within my blood
I try to imagine
Visualize a place
Far away...

Beyond the grid of the city
The stiff pine trees capped in thick snow
A clear icy stream
And bone white fields sculpted
Like oceans
Sun glinting off the undulating surface
The winter breeze
Shafts of yellow
My pale (frost-bitten) body yawing in
The dusted reeds

Long stalks
Lapping
Against my limbs (hoarfrost)
Burning like a thousand tiny cuts (of paper—)

My mind is racing
Up north the rivers
Over the land moving expansive tracts
Topographically freed...
Along the rivers (sluicing) fingers, soft meandering;

Exploring
The sheer lines of the bank,
The spires of the forest;
Songs half dormant
But
Imagining
The air in my lungs as the horizon of the sea

The Atlantic Ocean the Trinity Bay
Coffin Island
The Bay of Chub

An island like a cobbled cliff of
Emerald green along a wild frothing
Teal-grey ocean sentient—
A sloping
Escarpment
A giant circle of soft polished boulders,
Silvery, at the shore
Seagulls
Perched
And floating
Sweeping arcs in the wind
The salt hanging in the air

And wreaths of ancient looking kelp
Like netting trenched
Around its base

Sliding, wraiths,

Over the water, weightless in the surf

Wrapping
The sky.

—NAOMI SIMONE BORWEIN (she/her)

CITY-THIGHS

I disappeared because I was prey. Darting laughs, girl's teeth, and the men's ire all collecting in a cafe waiting for the next book. A passing affront leaving many confused. Intention becomes the lake filling with black. Every coffee ordered makes the wolf wince. Not knowing love. Without affect. Women graze by the boy staring into the mirror of the wall. An Aztec picks up a purring cat and feeds it only unpronounceable wisdom. I'm absorbed in human behavior. Studying how the veins on my hands are leading to every unseeable place on my body. Girls talk about the life they lead through a megaphone, as though I were not watching the contours of their arms and legs moving nervously, while she tells her friends why. Because I've destroyed Medusa and untangled her hair in my hands, made the coiled serpent rise within my spine until my circlet was wild. I've been unknown upon the earth. But now god has shown his beacon over my form and I am still ugly with truth. But sitting comely now, so that I cannot hide in my own shadow without the pale face of desire to forget me.

—HARRY EDGAR PALACIO (he/him)

until death

use my fingers as a toothbrush,
my distal bones gliding over
your gums (how you loved to
          feel me in your mouth).
mount my ribs in the entryway;
slam the front door! I will clasp
your jacket between bits of ossein.
this is your first appearance in weeks,
the door frame shuddering.
my carcass welcomes you home,
the dried-out leather of my skin
caressing your decaying form.
my clavicle scrapes against
the diner plate, and you choke
on leftover ligaments (let me be
          the last thing you taste).

—MAGGIE BOWYER (they/them)

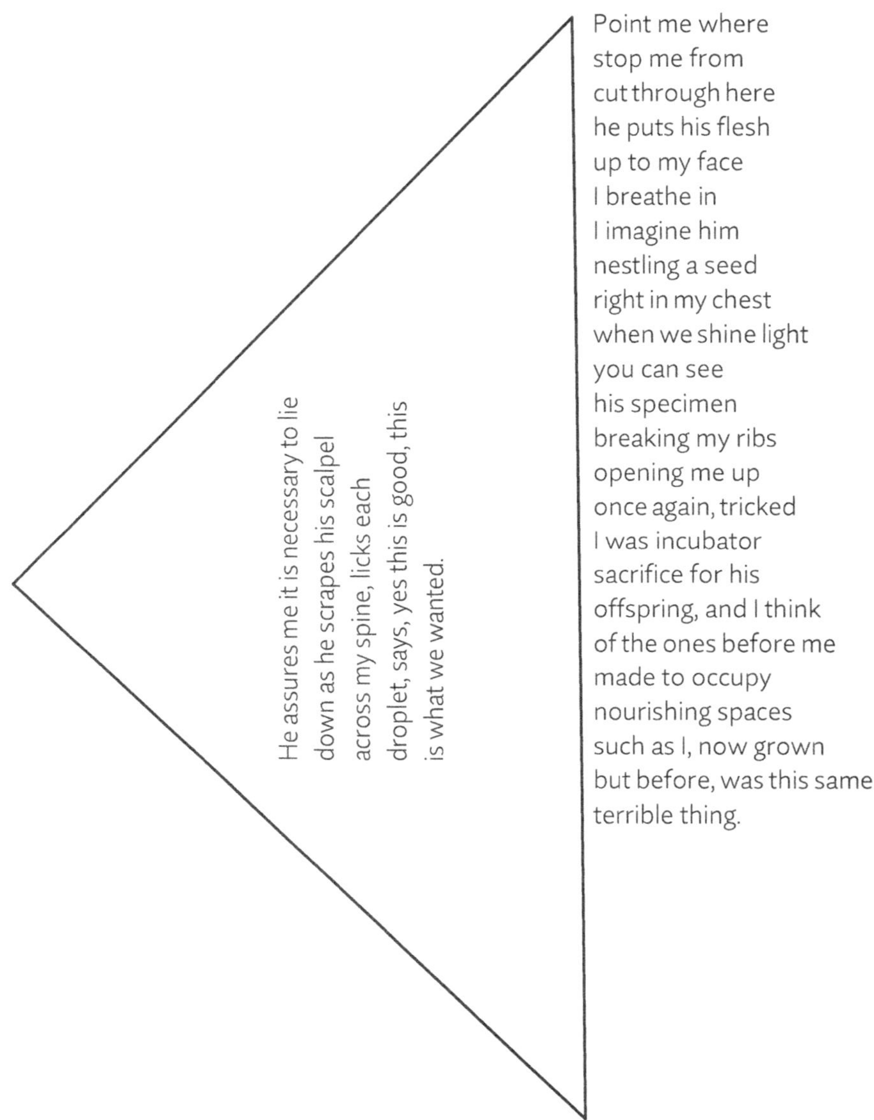

Point me where
stop me from
cut through here
he puts his flesh
up to my face
I breathe in
I imagine him
nestling a seed
right in my chest
when we shine light
you can see
his specimen
breaking my ribs
opening me up
once again, tricked
I was incubator
sacrifice for his
offspring, and I think
of the ones before me
made to occupy
nourishing spaces
such as I, now grown
but before, was this same
terrible thing.

He assures me it is necessary to lie
down as he scrapes his scalpel
across my spine, licks each
droplet, says, yes this is good, this
is what we wanted.

—MATEO PEREZ LARA (they/them)

ORGASM ORIGIN STORY (AFTER THE GARDEN OF EDEN)—TOMA ZBRIZHER (she/her)

Fleeing a father who couldn't get out of his own shame
they asked each other the first bottomless question:
W______?
You know, you have asked it before
Then second:
W______ m____?

Then all:

Wh_r_ __e t_ k_ys? Wh_t i_ _ l_ck? Wh_ is lo__ed?

Having exhausted all possibilities to justify a father's fa________[1]
they embraced one another for comfort and there
in the forgiveness of flesh
found a secret door beneath their touch
back inside bloom so human
it fooled a god

____

[1] possibilities-fail, failure, fatigue, fangirling, fangs, ~~fairness~~, favoritism,
fame, fading and so on

Post-Exposure Prophylaxis

Sick all over the shower,
half hangover, half medicine
if I'm honest, but when am I
honest? I was in that bedroom
again, that soft empty, that no-place.
Only the curtains witnessed:
hair in a stranger's fist, crescent
teeth marks on his shoulder, bruises
innumerable, random as stars
glittering in a glass pipe
from the windowsill, the box
still wrapped in plastic, mocking
from the bedside drawer,
the rope burn of crucifixion where wrists
kissed bed posts, the threat
of something wicked in my blood.
In stains on sheets. Caught on my tongue
with his name—what was it?
It is always better if the water
burns. I try to smoke the coiled snake
out of my body, wait for the strike
to crack the mirror. Already, decay:
it shows first around the eyes,
the hollowing ribcage. *Lucky.*
I am allowed to lose his name.
Lucky, lucky boy. A handful of blue
pills made for the labor of forgetting.

—BIRCH WILEY (they/them)

VALLEY HOSPITAL, RIDGEWOOD

Hours   days   months packed into hospital rooms,
a habitual persistence that turned an emergency ward into a fluorescent second home.
A rattling curtain backdrop against stark white walls, a comforting staple.
A tiny box window, letting in streaks of a world spinning without me.
Home   the smell of antiseptic in an over packed waiting room,
E.R. like a battle ground after the carnage   the plague   the inciting incident,
the sterile white light, a different kind of weapon.
A weight pressing down.

Back naked to hospital air, flesh so cold   my teeth speak in rhythm
hair reaching towards harsh light   frozen nasal capillaries burst.
Each visit, each second, hour,
blood drips into the neckline of a blue gown,
a macabre statement piece, complemented by the wails of babies with   croup   colic
chicken pox.

Admission is a release from the dry-heaving purgatory,
an *admission* that pain has a heartbeat and a life of its own   a blip or a heart monitor.
Admission is doubling over in a bed on wheels,
full of questions I don't have the words to ask   nurses that can't find a vein
surrounded by doctors with none of the answers.

—CASPER ORR (he/him)

Sometimes I dreamed them back to me.
My daddy, on and on about the right way
To do something, but in his own language.
Somehow I knew being understood
Was not his point. He kept going,
Fading into my wife who was
Weaving all over some road. Should I drive,
I asked my memory of her. I'm okay, it said,
Eyes deep with alien knowledge.

Sometimes they dreamed of me.
The morning after she died,
Sweeping the kitchen
To make myself function in some way,
And the tok-tok-tok
Of a ping pong ball, lost months ago
When she beat me in a game,
Bouncing in my dining room.

After the first few months,
They returned less often. Their mouths
No longer opened. What they didn't say
Had ceased to be a mystery.

I still dream them now and then,
Silent in some impossible place.
Smiles of wistful mockery.
Their eyes no longer meeting mine,
And then gone.

—ED BRICKELL (he/him)

PERHAPS THIS IS INHERITANCE

Some women learn to hang themselves on bedposts
before they sleep, scrape bruises off with a kitchen knife,
hide their grandmother's ring inside their breasts. My mother

told me pain is in the body and we live in the mind. Years
sand themselves against her bones. She taught me how
to play a hand dealt from a fraction of the deck. Some women

hide burns beneath their skin, patterns matching their living
room wallpaper. I once met a woman who kept a penkrife
folded in the hollow of her collarbone, said she knew how

to get it out with her mouth, said they never think of checking
for it there. As a child I was given a baseball bat that glowed
luminous pink. My little sister carved her name into its side.

—HOLLY ARCHIBALD (she/her)

I cannot break the code, lying in the dark
with memory—I have always forgotten
some key detail as I boiled in the moment,
clarity would flee me like a demon
exorcized by focus; like someone left
a magnifying glass out in the sun
& it burned a hole through my brain
& the smoke pressed against the face
of the sky until the yellow tendrils spelled out
"You gotta learn to pick your battles, Lu."

There is always an option to give up. There is grace
in hiding your wounds under a hat & retiring
to your bed midday. You cannot worry
that existing is eating holes in you when there
is still so much more of you to be had. & maybe

in the early-evening shade you will grieve
because you saw *love* once but had forgotten
to pack your trebuchet. You'll let the righteousness
swell in your marrow & splinter the false structure
of this subsistent reality as your heart-rate ticks down
into the tell-tale, lovesick, rabbit-footed thrum.

How many futures did you see
before you looked away?
The worlds inside reordering
the second you broke his gaze.

—LE FRANCIS (she/her)

TRANSTEMPORAL

We cut up Kane County
loop our bikes
through cornfields, water towers
and telephone poles, squash
Coke cans, wet newspapers
climb rooftops
to count the blinking lights
swallowed by the edge
of everything
to wish on stars gone cold
that we are already ancient
and have since migrated
to the fringes of Neptune's orbit
on Pluto or Eris or Arrokoth
in a future
where we ride hoverbikes
past icy bodies and space litter
on the Kuiper Belt.

—KALI JOY CRAMER (he/she)

FLASHBACKS AS ASTRAL PROJECTION

boundless sleep grants me astral clearance, in which i am a beam of light shattering in any direction, the chance of celestial spikes forming a body. it hurts to contain brightness and its insatiable faith as a cluster of dying stars. i exist in the expanse of a dream where doors are portals to every moment where you leave me shipwrecked, and mySelf becomes undone to a veil of white, 5-pointed. why do you mistake it as mist, as haunting? as in, why would i want to stay

where i am forced to live for you and the pain you put me through possesses me until i am the memory in which i wake up in motelblue light, the room vibrating with dust. you tell me you want me until it's you don't know how you feel, and you welcome reckless abandon before we take flight. i wish for the trespasses of your love, but time empties to despondent chasms of nothing, a crutch to rely on until something takes hold.

–tommy wyatt (he/they)

THOUGH YOU MIRROR

JT sliced into the mountains, so jagged, so fierce:
I see the man in the mountains and he says, *never!*
And shakes me with his finger.

JT up in the mountains, so jagged—so fierce—
I open my sleuth-box, but never thought I'd not want it—
my grandmother's diamond gleams like blood, like the past
And our brushed ghost does, too. A different back, a different face now.

Though you mirror sometimes, the scent of your death has dissipated.
Glue-ish particles swirled into water. You're over there now
and I'm up the other mountains, the ones with no face and my initials carved

like that deep, long cut on my back, once slammed into the mess on my
mother's apartment floor. My last name, over there, a not-so-gentle reminder
of my father's absence, of my singleness. I transition, I see the man

in the mountains in NH. I'm back, trembling fingers
on the other's face. I'm a kid, I'll be heading off
to Story Land, my one grand adventure.

I see him carved crisply—and he turns into you—
He tells me, *never, not ever again.*
He stops shaking me with his finger.

—JESS TOWER (she/they)

WE GREEN ADULTS—ALIX PERRY (they/them)

Back when the thickness
of a telephone pole's paper layer
still meant something,
I rode youth like a mechanical bull.
The shock of every buck
demanding its own debut, I walked
the neon-greased streets with my mouth open.
Bar-hoppers tossed grapes
onto my tongue, and I swallowed
them whole. The concrete
breathed beneath my feet, a life
I was not supposed to imagine.
Come summer, we green adults would
gather by the lake to watch
the foothill suburbs roll by on the
westbound wind. Candied
desolation, sarcastic wealth.
The beach was made of volcanic ash, and
when we emerged from
the water, that ghastly gray
coated our bodies with
a softer skin. I found a phone
book belly-up on the shore,
dialed the number for my future.
It just rang and rang.
Nonexistent or infinite. I shut
the book, buried it in
the freshwater sea, never
forgot those ten digits. A decade on, I tend
to call from the edge
of regret, no longer seeking
answers but affirmation of
their absence, a pattern of sound
& silence that says I couldn't
have known how this would end.

RESOLUTIONS

At the diner, bellies full, we order cherry pie.
The streets are mute with day old snow,
yellowing under the marigold moon.
You look at me and say,
It feels a lot like dying, this kind of life.
To which I reply,
But what do you know of dying?
To which you reply,
And what do you know of life?
Shift of body weight on vinyl, half a smile.
Outside, a crow cackles its omens
still too pale for this world.
The pie arrives, a bleeding heart on a paper plate.
We set to a slow plunder,
spoons clotting in the iron air.
Syrup sticks to everything
like a lukewarm plea
to carry on.

—ALINA KALONTAROV (she/her)

your house is all full. you never noticed
the blue blanket i stole, no, i rescued
from getting washed with *towels* and *clothes*,
all worse for the wear and less soft in the end.

your desk has no paperwork,
only *candies* and *candles* you buy in bulk
every fall, making sure your horde lasts.
i don't buy either, but i want them both.

glass balls hang from the ceiling
in every room. acquisitions over
a decade that hold dust
you have no energy to brush away.

claudette, bella, and *jeannette*, your hens
outside, eating dandelion greens
and corn you feed them to keep
them warm in the winter.

fiestaware you swear
isn't radioactive, only vintage.
this 1960s suburb fixed in your youth,
it isn't antique for you yet.

when you tell me to come home, i am strangled
by the diet and dessert *cookbooks* on every counter
the *mezuzot* in every hallway, every door
and the *shrine* to your sister that bleaches in the sun.

i want to tell you what you taught me
by living like this. when i have no room
to put *my coat* down in your house, i know
better than to take up space. your space.

where i can breathe, the walls are bare,
there are empty shelves for me to wipe clean,
i've built myself a life where i remind myself
the best way to keep a home is to keep nothing.

when there's nothing on the floor,
i can put *an air mattress* down
for a friend staying the night, or *a table*
for *a game* i hardly know the rules for.

i can fill my narrow space
with people, with life,
not lists of items, not permanent,
and not like the home i was raised in.

—ABBIE LANGMEAD (she/they)

LABORS OF HERACLES

Told my mother it was the cat knocked over
the concrete bird bath she'd just watched me topple
through the kitchen window. Called a boy some name
        on the playground once.

Slapped a girl across the face in middle school
I think underneath a Japanese maple
red light hanging over us. Cornered a girl
        in a high school stairwell,

tried to make her kiss me. Mocked someone in class
for pronouncing a word in accents I didn't
recognize. Knocked the closet door off its track with
        my body's high rage.

Broke the garage window stacking firewood.
Fucked that woman in that hotel room, our friend
asleep in the next bed. Fucked a friend's ex, too.
        Turned from a lover

when they turned my hand away, our bodies curled
spine to spine, sleepless in a strange apartment.
Lied and stole and cheated, blamed everyone else
        for the rot inside—

O litany of terrible deeds I don't
remember, which work still like a small machine
underneath memory. O litany
        of terrible deeds

I hope to see forgiven. O litany
of terrible deeds done against me I hope
to forgive. My mother helped me stand the bird bath
        back on its stone feet.

—BIRCH WILEY (they/them)

IN ANOTHER LIFE PT II

in another life

I storm in and take all the jewelry
The bed is unmade
(which it never was)

And he changed the bathroom colors
You liked the blue bathroom, I think you liked blue because it felt like
your first life

Anyway in another life
I'm sneaking my way into the room
With ceilings high enough to touch
you

And I run away with a case of your treasures
And a grin that won't leave me
(even though my knees are threatening to roll me down the hill)
And maybe he's even chasing me

But the rubies, the sapphires, and a hundred kisses—
Oh we make it every time.

—STACEY MANOS (she/her/ella)

December 21, the longest night of the year
arrives in a slow succession of lengthening shadows,
and we are thrown into a landscape of unshakable
sleep, hoar-frosted dreams, unrealized possibility.
At mid-day, the earth turns ashen with twilight,
the distant sun a reminder of past lives,
those bright summer days bursting with sweet
berries, ripe promises born year after year.
In the yearning dark, we stretch our arms toward
the falling light if only to hold its yellow heat
between our hands for a moment.
If only to hear a jubilant chorus of birdsong
echo through these dying hours.
To feel the gentle surge of green born in the underground,
tenacious as the tree reaching ever higher
toward the unseen.

—CHRISTEN LEE (she/her)

FICTION

Your mother tells you there is a new litter of pups in the greenhouse. You rush out to see them in your sleep clothes—sweatpants and a hoodie—stopping quickly to force your naked feet into rubber boots. You should not be in the garden after dark (*Rule #3: avoid the garden after sundown*), but you want to see them before their skin stops glowing, typically one to two hours after hatching. Your mother allows an exception to the rule, provided you bring a candle with you. The sky is yet bright enough to barely illuminate the footpath, and you move swiftly and quietly and the flame in your hands dissuades the tendrils that might otherwise snake onto the path and loop your ankles. Approaching the corner of the garden bed, you can see light coming from underneath clods of dirt. A slight movement, soft attempt to writhe.

The Mother, looming over her bright babies, dark violet tree of muscle and carapace, rots already. Great sheaths of husk peel from her trunk. Her many pitcher mouths, ringed with dark and deadly teeth, are slack and gaping. Her spirit has moved entirely into the bodies of her offspring.

Crouching, you brush away a layer of black dirt, and count six. Your hand skims the luminescent skin, taut with light. No shell yet: in their most vulnerable state. They are tied to one another by a thin white web of root-lace.

You dig for the runt. In a litter this big, there is guaranteed to be one. There—suffocated beneath its siblings—is a smaller, dimmer bulb. This seventh pup is the size of your palm and already tinged with the yellow edges of death.

Your mother calls to you from the back door, asking for the count. Without thinking, you snatch the runt from the dirt. Delicate roots snap sickeningly and shrink back into themselves. You shove it into your sweatshirt pocket and rub the dirt off your hands. When you reenter the yolk-flood of porchlight, your mother's silhouette asks, "How many?" and you reply, "Six."

***

You are thinking about Rule #2: *NO plants, monstrous or otherwise, may enter the house.* The house is large and square, surrounded by protective rings. First, a wrought-iron fence separates the house from the greenhouse, then there is the greenhouse itself (misty, glassy, glowing), and finally, a tall brick wall blocks sight of the street. The city outside is wonderfully smoggy and loud compared to the silent buzz of the greenhouse and perfect stillness of the house, and you often long for it. Your mother does not let you wander in the streets alone, though you think that might change as you get older. You turn 16 in a month, and the curfew has not loosened yet.

There is not a single living thing inside the house besides you and your mother. You have never been allowed a bouquet, let alone a pet. Once, when you were very young, a seed rode inside on the back of your mother's shoe. You came downstairs the next morning to the smell of burning rubber; your mother stood in front of the kitchen sink, lighter in hand. In the sink was a metal bucket in which her sneaker sat smoldering. A small but thick root protruded from the shoe's canvas, curled like a beautiful lock of hair. Eaten by flames, the root shriveled into a desiccated umbilical cord. That was when your mother wrote Rule #5: *outside shoes must be kept separate from inside shoes.*

***

Your mother has told you many times that there are always more pups, or seeds, produced than will survive. This has always been hard for you to accept. You have recurring dreams about very small birds, the size of bees, that you crush as you attempt to cradle. Other times you dream about transparent, miniscule mice, who expire from the softest touch of your fingertips.

You can't remember what experience seeded the extreme feeling of debt within you, and you are grateful to your brain for wiping it from your memory. The small, flimsy-skinned animals are all that remain. Somehow you understand that keeping the bulb alive is some final form of payment, made all the more valuable by the fact that it is the only thing about you your mother does not know.

***

The pup is in a cereal bowl, with a small amount of water, on your desk under the window. Its siblings are visible, tendrils crawling up the Mother, their small roots determinedly wrapping around her old ones. When you hear your mother on the stairs, you shove the bowl under your bed and some water sloshes out.

103

You are gratified to find that the runt has lost its yellow tinge, and that it reaches roots up the side of your bedside table to drink from last night's water glass when it has drunk its bowl dry. Now that it is hardier, you take to carrying it around in your sweatshirt pocket.

***

One evening, you wake up in your bed from an unplanned nap, curled on your side, with blankets thrown to the floor. Your skin is coated in dried sweat, and you are tired in a way that makes full consciousness evasive. You had been dreaming of walking around town in the sun, remembering suddenly that you had thrown your pet goldfish loose into your purse; you panicked, trying to dig through the contents quickly but gently, imagining the wet skin of your fish adhering to the lining of the bag.

A dull pain radiates through your body, starting from the pit of your stomach. It sobers you slightly. You remember the pup, a small bulge fast asleep in your pocket. Sitting up, you reach to remove it, and find that you cannot. Your sweatshirt as well resists your attempt to pull it up. Your brain floods cold, then hot: the bulb's roots have woven themselves through the fabric of your hoodie and attached to the soft skin of your stomach.

You leave your room and walk slowly to the small library that is also on the second floor, gently supporting the bulb's weight with one hand so the roots do not pull painfully. Your mother is bent over a large book of her own botanical sketches. She looks up, and asks you what is wrong.

She isn't mad. You are sitting on the library's broad wooden table, which is normally covered in books. An evening glow comes in through the skylight. Large fabric scissors have chopped away your hoodie's front pocket, and the pup is exposed. You hover a hand over the plant protruding from your stomach. The bulb is full and healthy looking, nearly the same size as its siblings. It seems to have grown even in the last hour, resting on top of your thighs. You feel it react to the heat of your hand, inhaling towards your skin. You know better now than to try and coax its roots from your body; it only tightens its grip in a way that sends shocks of pain up your abdomen. Your mother brews you a cup of sweet-smelling maroon tea and tells you to wait. She goes downstairs to the bigger library.

You understand, in the back of your brain, what it would mean to seek help from the outside world. The plants—and your mother—would be taken away. Rule #1: *No visitors in, no plant matter out.* What would happen to you then?

You wait for a few minutes, then grab the fabric scissors and hop quietly off the table, one hand supporting the bulb. Soon, you are outside, a silhouette on the porch again. Bulb in one hand, shears hanging at your side in the other. Your bare feet feel the hot night dirt, and Rule #4 skims past your consciousness: *Always wear close-toed, rubber shoes.* The thickness of the greenhouse air touches your stomach. Root tentacles slither onto the path and drag across your ankles as you walk.

The Mother is disintegrating. Her pitcher mouths droop to the ground. The pups feed on her scraps. They are doing well, already several inches tall, starting to form their scaly outer layer. Once they have fed enough, they will crawl to separate parts of the yard before rooting, to avoid eating each other. They raise themselves from their meal and vibrate quietly at your approach.

You kneel in dirt, resting the bulb on your legs again, just out of reach of the pup's quivering mouths. You wriggle slowly out of your hoodie, pulling it forward so you can see where the roots thread through the fabric and enter your skin. Shirtless, kneeling in the garden, you, root by root, begin snipping, careful to miss your stomach. At the cut ends, your blood mixes with a milky white sap. It is only when you are halfway through that you realize your mother is beside you. The last root snaps as the bulb rolls off your lap, and you gasp in pain. Your mother wraps a towel around your bare shoulders. She pulls the limp bulb from beneath your discarded hoodie and approaches the tree. The siblings quake in excitement, stretching upwards. She places it at the base of the roots, but as the pups turn inward to feast, they are interrupted by a sudden movement from the Mother as one of her massive mouths turns on the ground and engulfs the runt in a cavern of teeth.

***

Over the next few days, the root stubs sticking from your stomach shrivel and are expelled. Your skin heals quickly, though it will remain tender for weeks, and you need your mother's help to reach higher shelves. The scars are in the shape of a sunburst, or a spider.

You cannot blame your mother for being more watchful of you lately. She accompanies you during your chores in the garden and stares in deep thought across the dinner table. Often, you see her make notes in a notebook labeled '*Hybrids.*' She adds a rule to the list on the fridge: #6: *The ones who must go, let them.*

Three of the pups, now scattered throughout the garden, reach adulthood. They turn a grungy purple, collect water in their mouths. In your dreams you wriggle beside them in the dirt, watch your skin glow from the inside as you are born, watch with an unknown feral hunger your mother taking notes on the other side of the garden, watch your translucent fingers felt and shed like leaves to the earth and your mother collect them gently in a wide ceramic bow; after diligent experimentation it is found they carry no properties of healing or poison but, if boiled in water, make for a cup of saccharine purple tea.

—MAYA FRIEDMAN (she/they)

She felt lucky to be living in this park. There was no envy towards those living in that park with grass and trees, whatsoever. After all, she had her own shower in the car park and had been told by many announcements just how fortunate that made her. It was tall, svelte and powerful. She was content to let it shape her appearance as it saw fit, rush its force down her, and leave its scent on her for the day.

She lived—like everyone else who was still alive—under the almost-glare of the concave, transparent glass disk that was balanced on her head. Like everyone else's, her disk was tilted at the Benevolent Angle. A rather unpleasant lever sat at the bottom of her trunk, but she made sure the ghastly thing was always covered by a gun cloth or a face wipe. A long time ago, the hand of a woman with short, spiky hair and silver triangles for eyes had held hers, stroked her quivering knuckles. Her lever had been pulled. What remained of her was a red leather coat, singed from the flames, which also rested in the trunk.

The morning was like the bottom of a crisp packet: shiny and sticky. She went to shower, only to find one of the tiles stacked along the bottom of the shower had come ajar. Curious, she gave it a tug. The tile clattered onto the concrete, bruising one corner.

She balled her fists and forked her tongue. Peered into the cavity. It was all of her: old hair, skin, gunk, snot, gathered excitedly like fans at a concert. She was the heir to a kingdom!

This basin concealed beneath the shower had become completely blocked. The smell stretched her eyes wide. Fetid and pungent—up her nose travelled a purple and black marbled egg. She pressed up close to the gap. Brown scum lacquered the enamel. Thick, ropey netting stretched in hammocks between the walls. A gurgling, greenish pudding pushed up against the central, vertical pipe.

As she beheld it, she realised how much she'd lost over the years. How much the shower had taken from her. She returned the tile to its original place and made a small, oval smudge of grime on the ivory tile with the tip of her third finger.

"You must never return to that place, or great trouble will befall you," the shower told her sternly. She avoided the shower head's sharp expression and didn't step into its arms like she usually did, bracing for its cold cuddle.

Instead, she returned to her trunk, stroking its gilded lock. It had been a while since she'd felt admired. The shower expressed delight for her, but only when she was freshly washed and pleasant as a cucumber.

The air turned into flashing hot foil. Time to go to work. Unusually heavy and happy, the drips of boiling sun juice hardly stung her skin. The disk sat jauntily on her head. She'd never felt particularly fearful of the large saucer. She was sure the Blit Angle would never befall her glass and always made sure to turn away if she ever saw another disk swivelling, to cover her ears and walk on. It wasn't becoming to see a sun ray sharpen into a pencil of fire, bury into someone's head and incinerate them. She had better ways to spend her time. She kept her disk squeaky clean and her hair coiffed. No soul would destroy her, no matter how slack she was at work.

She returned to the park at the end of the working day, the heat scrunched into high-pitched corners. As she picked her way through her neighbours, she noticed they were avoiding her gaze. A drop of sympathy for the shower wet her brow. Perhaps she should have let it clean her up this morning, after all.

A jangling noise wrapped itself around her neck and pulled tighter and tighter, the closer she was to her trunk. She knelt down, coughing, sweating copiously, and pushed the fleshy, red, and burnt hide of a jacket to one side. Her lever. Pealing so loudly, you could imagine someone's skin doing the same thing under a concentrated sun ray. Her destiny: to murder someone else, to turn their disk. Without warning, a large cube of sick leapt out of her throat and hopped away. A myriad of ants scurried over the melting tarmac towards it.

The rope, distracted by the cube and its followers, loosened, and she tore it off her neck, then scrambled to her feet, dragging the coat with her, and flew over to the shower, accidentally sending her disk flying off her head and smacking onto the car park ground. It cracked but skittered away, across painted lines and underneath a brown car. She jumped into the shower, eyeing its impeccable tiles, pulled down her pants and peed. The shower sputtered, and she rubbed the red coat against its head, then pulled the fork out from her tongue, bent it and jammed it against the switch, immobilizing it completely. Reaching down, she grabbed the tile with the oval smudge, slipped it out of place, then pushed her head against the crack until it widened to accommodate it. Her shoulders followed, then her hips, feet and finally her hands and the coat. She pulled its tails in, and then, yanked the tile up. There was no time to say farewell to the park.

Not even to the disk, whom she had complicated feelings for. It did look good, after all. It was only really when you were involved with its nasty side that it became a nuisance.

Nobody ever came looking for her. Perhaps the subjugated shower and broken disk had unnerved those who would enforce the logic of the lever. Perhaps she no longer existed, her muck having swallowed her away from the walls of the world. She didn't care, either way, since she was surrounded by her scum, by all of herself, not the thick-skinned, verdurous version the shower sent her to work as. Her head filled with gunky water and bulging eggs and she trailed knuckles through old, lacy hair. Thus, she devoted herself to the practices of stretching and sipping through sewers, discovering the infinite delights of sludge from underneath the shower basin for the next three hundred and thirty-three years.

—LIZ YARWOOD (she/they)

Iga steps outside of herself. Upright rather than supine, she moves to the side of her sleeping body, then tiptoes away from the bed and towards the door, being careful not to wake her duplicate self. Fortunately, she's a heavy sleeper.

Iga has never been one to wake in the night. She has never been one to miss, even snooze, an alarm. To her, sleep is an efficient deal struck by a board of expert negotiators. Since about 15, she has known exactly what she needs: 6.5 hours. Not 7. Not 6. The amount's enough to function well, but also raises a bar slightly above her, which her days always need. She's at her most professionally, socially, and emotionally productive when her executed actions are slightly behind the next person's. She thrives when she has regular reasons to be slightly disappointed in herself without major detriment. She's most herself when her day is a conveyor belt of opportunities to improve—to the small extent that she feels better but that these improvements go unnoticed by the strangers and friends around her.

Iga closes the bedroom door behind her, quietly. She doesn't know what would happen if she made enough noise that it woke her. Would the unconscious version of her become conscious, and she then fade into the air? Would she return to supine, from wherever she stands? Would the responsibility to put things back into place fall on someone or something else, so she simply turns off and shuts down?

Iga decides that the best course of action is a cup of coffee and a bite to eat. She won't be able to get anything done until she raises her energy levels. The premise of the hybrid, real/dream version of her small townhouse unnerves her, so she seeks breakfast outside. Maybe she would prepare the coffee and the cup would disintegrate in her fingers. Maybe she would pour the coffee into her mouth but nothing would go down her throat. Or maybe the props in the hybrid house are as unreal and dreamed as her, so they would all function with a consistent internal logic—*working*, because she's living, inexplicably.

But the threat of waking herself remains. Iga decides to test the potential of the dreamscape beyond these four walls.

***

Iga's time outside is brief. The space is a vessel, transporting her to a new interior: a small café closer to the city centre.

The café is a hive of consumer activity. Eyes scan the menu and compare item values. Other people know their orders and stride up to the counter, so confident in the knowledge of what the card reader will instruct them to pay that they don't look at it, their eyes on their phone screens. Some add snacks and pastries to their drinks order, throwing extra donations at an unseen force as if the gesture signals free market agency or *actual* power.

Everyone's moving. Inside the café, but also outside, because Iga can see the city streets from her window seat as she warms her hands around a steaming cup of flat white. She wonders if this perpetual motion is a condition of the dreamscape. No-one stands still or sits still. People seem unable to. She's the only exception.

Iga experiments with this rule. As a barista takes a pair of used cups from a nearby table back to the counter, Iga asks her to stop for a moment. Iga asks her to literally stop moving for a moment. She looks sideways at Iga, confused but used to a disposably strange encounter with a member of the general public. The look suggests that Iga's request is tame compared to some of the things she's been asked while working in this busy metropolitan hospitality venue.

"No, please, I'm serious. Can you stand still for a second? Prove to me that you can."

"I'll be right with you," the barista offers.

Five minutes later, the manager comes over. The manager's an overzealous middle-aged man who seems to have worked at the café for too long to still transparently enjoy it this much. He's the kind to treat a weekday rush hour like a military operation, a customer question like an existential enquiry.

But he brushes off Iga's question too. It's probably cause it's weird. Harmlessly so. It's not the kind of weird question to warrant ejection from the café—an action this manager would also relish taking seriously, Iga suspects—but the kind it's convenient to pretend he's too busy to respond to. He imagines that something has caught his eye to justify speeding off in a different direction. Then he invents instructions to give the shift's second and third baristas when he's back at the counter. Then he pushes through the metallic silver door taking him to the staff back room.

For the rest of her time at the café, the baristas avoid Iga's eye. She doesn't see the manager again.

An hour after asking them to stop moving, Iga leaves.

She clears her croissant crumbs and throws away her cup on the way out.

Back outside, she tries asking a few passersby to stop moving.

They look at Iga like she's grown a second head.

She has witnessed rehearsals of this scenario herself, many times.

People will always look at a lone woman in a busy city asking questions, seeking answers to alleviate her confusions, as if she's crazy.

It's too real to be a dream.

***

Iga wonders if there has been a malfunction, if she's dreaming on the wrong side. She entertains, then believes in, the possibility that the framework for her unconscious state is askew. She disappears down the rabbit hole of *dreamer accidentally stuck in reality*. She buys into the idea that she's the only one dreaming and has no intention of returning or re-selling the belief. She comes to terms with the idea that *she's* the anomaly.

Iga's belief is disrupted by the constant motion thing, though. There are further problems on public transport, which she uses to test her theory. What happens when the *things* are moving—are people?

Iga takes a northbound underground train across the city. Everyone's still moving. She wants to ask strangers to try and stop but they wouldn't hear her over the competing engines, traction motors, brakes, and wheels rolling on the rails. Roughness and irregularity on the wheel and rail surfaces ensure that Iga cannot be heard. She's silenced by the city.

Iga can only watch as people in the carriage around her pace, hop on one or two legs, twirl their bodies as they grip handrails, tap their legs in time with their private music, or shuffle their feet to avoid being stepped on by the crowds of individuals they don't know going to different destinations for unknown purposes.

It doesn't help that Iga unwittingly selected the underground line that doesn't have seats, to accommodate a larger carriage capacity. Standing still is more unrealistic than sitting still.

***

Iga's daughter is somewhere. Somewhere in her original reality—which she expects to return to when she wakes—awaits her four-year-old daughter. Iga's the only one responsible for the child, because the child's father left four years ago. The child is the only one responsible for Iga, because Iga's father died five years ago and her mother died eight years ago.

***

Iga notices a development when she's back outside, after the unsuccessful train test.

Iga realises that the sky is moving, like everyone, except her, unless she chooses to. The sky is slowly moving downward and closer to the ground, as if a theatre curtain is coming down in stages. This must not be reality. Iga learns this because she stops to focus on the sky for several minutes. The sky moves down gradually, but the movements accumulate and create a significant new position after enough staring.

Iga learns more from exteriors than interiors here—wherever and whatever *here* is. Here, the outside world proves more trustworthy: the inverse of her life on the other side, where she and her daughter maximise the happiness of a private, sheltered life by staying indoors and playing, laughing, and daydreaming the hours away together.

In that alternative *here*, Iga tells her daughter that no-one can touch them. Here, she often thinks but keeps to herself, the father she will never tell her daughter about cannot touch them.

Iga and her daughter have a designated safe place to escape outside to. They call it "The Garden", but really it's a small patch of grass attached to their home's private patio—11 square feet to be exact. Iga escapes here to breathe when she needs a moment to herself, sneaking a quick cigarette and a lungful of air while her daughter plays. Her daughter escapes here to extend the boundaries of her play—using green turf and blue sky to justify new worldbuilding. The outdoor space has fences taller than her daughter on three sides, so Iga lets her daughter roam free, granting her

113

opportunities for solitude because she suspects that even a four-year-old needs them.

For her daughter, The Garden unlocks new possibilities. Her fantasies can take flight without the limits of a roof. Her solitary games with her toys can write their own rules without the obstacle of narrative logic. On the 11 square feet of grass, she can be anyone. She can do anything. She doesn't need to share these particular someones and somethings with her mother. These stories remain hers. Her mother keeps a longer, more complex story to herself—unlike her daughter, she'll have to share this, one day.

The idea of returning to the hybrid house fills Iga with dread. She doesn't know what steps she must take back at the gateway, if it even is one, to get home.

—GEORGE OLIVER (he/him)

They said it was best that I wasn't left alone.

It's what they said. The blurry men arrived in vehicles with flashing lights and voices muffled by the ring of sirens and chlorinated water still trapped in my ears. A strange gurgling drowning tinnitus. Ring, gurgle, gurgle, ring, ring...

No, I should not be alone, though I want to be.

Matt brings me back to his house. I lay in bed with him. He rubs my back. I touch his chest. His hands are on my face, he wipes my hair away. It looks wet and feels dry. Our lips are against each other's skin, not kisses, just moths beating against a flame. Trying to burn, but my wings are damp. Nothing will catch fire.

Nothing is sexual. It's necessary. It's movement.

Mindless.

Numbing.

Hands.

Mouths.

Crying.

I'm not alone, but I feel alone. It's now, and it's the rest of my life. It's impossible to comprehend.

He was too young to be out there by himself. I knew this. I know this. I should have been there.

Around 4 a.m. Matt seems to sleep. My eyes close, his breath is slow. His eyes don't move under their lids. He's not dreaming. I don't sleep. My fingertips are puffy with slivers and pool water. The bottoms of my feet sting. Memories of a hot deck, and then, standing on crabgrass.

So many little deaths. My throat is filled with pushpins and chemical water.

I wind my hair around my finger and weave the end into my mouth, the way I did when I was four. My hair is dry but still stiff with hair product and pool water. It tastes like chorine. It tastes like yesterday

My breath—is stale with bourbon and blame.

Matt's eyes start to move under his eyelids, they dart back and forth in a little dance. He is asleep, which seems impossible but it's true. He isn't moving or snoring. Just still. Just gone.

I was not supposed to be left alone, but here I am.

At 4 a.m. everything in this neighborhood smells like rotted lilacs and car exhaust. It smells like apartments with low ceilings and narrow hallways. I close my eyes and my hands reach for something that's not here.

My fingers poke at Matt's back like he is a hallucination. I am not alone. I am alone. I'm not alone. I am alone.

He doesn't wake.

My parent's house is 3.4 miles from here. Shorter as the crow flies. But. I'm no crow. I'm just crunchie, chlorine hair and—nothing...I am nothing.

Matt doesn't wake up when I leave the bed; I wish he would, I wish he were with me as I lift his car keys off their sensible hook near the door.

I wish he were with me when I put the car into drive and my stinging foot presses on the gas pedal.

3.4 miles in pseudo-suburban 4 a.m. time takes a little under 11 minutes. I don't remember stop signs or easing my foot off the brake for an opossum.

I remember the taste of my hair, chlorine. I remember the smell of my breath, stale bourbon.

There is nothing else until I am here. My parents never kept anything of note in the shed—nothing I cared about, until now. I wish my father was with me when I see the ax, again—for the first time since I was a kid.

An old rusty ax doesn't need to be protected. It's not a gun, and I'm not Lizzie Borden looking to kill my parents, at least not then—and no, not now either. I can't kill them, even though it's their fault...too.

My victim is an above-ground-four-foot pool. Everybody hates them.

Walking on crabgrass sounds like knives on silk, but it doesn't feel like anything. "Dad, how should I swing this ax?"

He's not here.

I can't feel the grass, I smell the chlorine, I hear the sirens, and even now the ax isn't heavy; it's just there, waiting to be used.

Metal on metal.

When I was ten, I begged for an inground pool but no, no—we are all guilty now.

I've never played sports, but when I swing the ax into the side of the pool, I feel like I've found my calling. It's just a little dent, but I swing back and hit again. I am a mother with a child trapped under a car. I am a woman who can do anything. I am a hero.

Aluminum is not stronger than I am.

The third time I hit, the side buckles, it has two little holes that cry, that weep—they mourn.

Again.

Again.

Again.

This pool mourns with no end.

The muscle under my right shoulder starts to burn and then dissolve into nothing.

I Swing. Connect. Swing again.

I feel my elbow bounce back, it's out of place. My right shoulder is now two inches lower than the left. The crying pool weeps, then pours, then gives up.

So do I.

When the water rushes out, it feels like a wall comes crashing into my chest. It knocks me on my ass.

Water splashes over me, it creeps into my mouth, my throat. It tastes like plastic and memories. Like inner tubes and waterproof sunscreen. It tastes like a bad decision and regret. It tastes like everything I have lost. I keep coughing, I don't let it in.

That would be too easy.

Crabgrass starts to feel like moss and bittersweet yesterdays. Then 52,000 gallons of water rushes over it, and yesterdays don't matter.

I am here. I let it beat against my chest, my ax is in my hand and then it's not. Like a lover being swept out to sea. The ax ends up in the neighbor's yard. I hold onto the earth. My puffy fingers are in the dirt, I think I am holding onto an ant's dens and willow roots. I let the water take me and spit me out.

The men with the sirens and flashing lights were right—

I should not be alone.

—JENNIFER ANNE GORDON (she/they)

The fireworks exploded, bright spermlike streaks in night air, and the music roared like rhythmic thunder, until you escaped outside—which Patty had done, sweaty beads on her back from the close and pulsing room. Outside: the humid sky a moist film landing everywhere.

Earlier that day she'd swallowed the vast expanse of white beach, better than Ohio at Christmas with its gift shops and pizza parlors. Her breath moving through her: wide and big-bellied, remembering her body.

Out on the deck, Russell chortled next to her, his seventh drink in his hand (she counted these days, more out of some illusion of control, when she knew there was nothing she could do to stop it) and bounced up and down imploringly, his eyes exaggerating desperation for her to join him, before he swam back into the crowd inside.

Patty chose the quiet here, the still in the palm fronds, flapping in breeze. The air picked up, and she stood on the stone ledge, fascinated by how the fronds also danced, even when the wind lashed and whipped. Her dress lifted up at the bottom and hurled upward, wetted and waving in the wind.

Now she could hear guests around her commenting on the gusts, running back to their rooms or other shelter. Then there was the sudden downpour. She streaked for the closest door, the glass front of the main lobby, warm with light and smooth tan couches.

That's when it hit, cool and slow and deadly like a shark, the water losing its shoreline and spreading like a hand across the lawn, over the ledges, everything soaked as a bathtub; the winds now wild with dance, manic. Everywhere, shrieks. She looked desperately for Russell in the moving bodies but the power lines were down and there was only darkness and the surprise of a moon behind the haze, opaque light.

***

Running, running with everyone, the elevators jammed, the lines of people stringing up the open stairs to get to their rooms, as if closing a door behind them would end it, return normalcy like a light switch. All she can think to do is hum, hum the song her mother taught her in dark Midwest nights, the power outages in the dead of winter and the sound of her younger sisters, scared and wordless. Humming was better than gossip and worry, kept the mind in its centered place, kept things clear.

Finding her way to the back of the bungalow, water sloshes all around her feet, shoes squishing. Somewhere, a siren. She clutches at the glass door in the back, to pull it open first so it won't shatter in the rising pressure of water, hoping her forgetfulness has left it unlocked.

Yes: a slight click of the mouth of the lock releasing its teeth and the door glides open, now the floor filled with water—was this better or worse? Her ear, shoved to the ground by the force of new water, her face submerged briefly as if listening to the roots of earth; then yanked to the edge of the room by wet flame, the lick of that violent water.

Her things: on the floating bed, the clothes thrown there earlier while changing, the undecided dressing for evening cast in shoes and scarves. Standing again, dripping, she's wobbly-kneed in water, piling all she can carry up to the extra loft bed, up the ladder. Up, up. Her breath heaving like that wind, feet slippery on the rungs.

Until the ladder goes too, beneath her, swimming in the water. And she is in the raised loft, clinging to her piles of clothes. Clinging to breathing above that water line.

***

It feels like hours of this, the chaos and sounds. Crying, screams, water. A metallic groan of the structure itself being strangled and fighting to right itself. Then the wood of the loft begins to float, unmoored. As it moves, there is the feel of bodies, churning underground and floating up and past like bath toys. Until she loses consciousness, her body wet like a flat sail and drifting.

***

Light, the aftermath—a surprise, but soft like breathing; a sense that life has continued on. Somehow it is morning. Her body sways with the water, on top of a piece of that wood, but the water shallower, just a ripple now beneath her, pushing her back and forth like a cradle. All around, washed up bodies, some coughing, some ghost-still and pale, the life gone.

There are men in orange uniforms with helmets and hotel staff in black, picking through corpses and crying children. The bellies of palm fronds upturned and ragged, stripped from their limbs, everywhere. When they find her she is numb and wordless, a cry caught in her throat.

120

****

Days later, there is nothing to take on that plane. Her body is bruised like ripe fruit. The hotel has rounded them up like stray cats, to an open center, taken their names and used a generator to pull up records on computers, rendering identities through old maps of themselves: arrival dates, scanned credit cards and passports, the skins of civilization. Enough to send them traveling, homeward, cut loose like beads.

Whiplash: the cry in her low and buzzing like shaken fizz. Now, the plane, carrying her toward landlocked Ohio, its familiar snow and taxi cabs, bars' neon lights, the places that remember her. She has not found Russell, no one has. They say it will be days before they know where everyone is. Will they ever know?

****

In the climate control of the cabin, Patty unpacks the plastic-packaged blanket, turns the air to off, feels the surprise of choice again. When the flight attendant offers her champagne, she accepts, her lips linking this sip to days earlier: a different body, a different time, that line that can separate then from now like a knife, cool and quiet as the dark; one moment from the next like a cloak slipped over unwashed clothes.

—AS AUBREY (she/her)

I wake up knowing that today is the day.

I close my bedroom door, but not all the way. Completely shutting it would attract unnecessary attention. Privacy isn't allowed in the little red house. He knows all, he sees all. Like an evil god. I try to carve out places of my own. The closet in my room juts out, creating a small alcove. The head of my twin bed is tucked inside that alcove. The narrow space between the bed and the wall of the alcove is hidden from view of anyone who happens to walk by, making it my own private space. If anyone should approach my bedroom door, I'll hear the sound of their steps before they appear and have plenty of time to hide what mustn't be revealed. This spot in the alcove is the perfect place to plan my father's most untimely death.

Today, I am a chemist with a steady hand—I am a mad scientist with a perfect plan. Feeling mischievous, I rub my palms together, reveling in the wickedness of what I'm about to do. He'll never see it coming. If all goes well, it'll be over before he can stop it.

Actually, I prefer chemist to mad scientist. I'm not the one who's mad, after all. I am angry, it's true, and have been for so long I can hardly remember anything else, but I am not mad. I am a man of science with precise, measured moves; my hands are capable of remaining steady no matter what. They will not tremble in fear. Of course, I understand that I am nothing but a boy with very little power, but I can feel a new strength in these unflinching hands of mine and take a moment to admire them.

They have already done most of the hard work. There's a long white scar across my left hand; it starts between my thumb and index finger but takes a sudden turn to cross the top of my wrist, like someone tried to cut me open with a jagged knife that suddenly slipped. Gazing further down along my arm, I can see faded yellow bruises that remind me of something putrid. But I can't think of those mysterious marks right now. I have a job to do.

I take a deep breath and close my eyes; when I open them, I'm able to focus my full attention on the task at hand. I pull the plastic sandwich bag from beneath my mattress; it holds my supply of crushed sleeping pills. Cradling it in one hand as I lift it up and down, testing the weight of my supply, I wonder if it's enough. I need more than I've ever used before. I'm not just putting him to sleep for the evening like I've done in the past. I'm putting him to sleep for good this time.

The baggie's quite full, but I can't take any chances. Although I've assumed the role of chemist, I have no idea how many sleeping pills it takes to kill a man. Fifteen? Twenty? I've heard of people swallowing a bottle of sleeping pills when they want to off themselves, so that's a good place to start. There's at least a bottle's worth of crushed pills inside the bag already, and I have an unopened one to work with as well. But as I think back to all the times I've drugged my father over the past year or so, I remember the constant fear that he'd notice something was off if I poured too much of the white powder into his drink. Before, I only wanted to knock him out for the night so he'd leave us alone. And it worked. Finally, I found something that worked! He fell asleep on the couch much earlier than normal and never noticed a thing. By the time he woke the next morning, he didn't suspect anything out of the ordinary had occurred the night before. If he had a headache or felt groggy, he blamed the booze. He had no idea what I'd done because I was so careful, slipping only small amounts into his drink at a time when he went to the bathroom, quickly stirring it around with my finger before he got back. The first time, I basically held my breath until he fell asleep, terrified he might notice what I'd done. What if the pills made his whiskey taste different? Or might he notice a slight discoloration in the amber liquid?

But it worked out just fine. By the third time, my confidence had increased, so I poured more into his drink, making sure he'd pass out even faster. Once, I accidentally spilled more than I meant to inside his cup and panicked when I couldn't make it dissolve fast enough. Even then, when he took a sip, he didn't notice a thing. That night, I wondered if I might have accidentally killed the bastard; secretly, I hoped that I had. Yet, to my great disappointment, he woke the following morning. Coughing and spitting from all the smoking but still very much alive.

I've also drugged his cans of beer, which is trickier in some ways but easier in others. Getting the rocky powder inside without leaving a trace is more challenging since the opening of the can is so much smaller, but once it's in, I just shake the beer around, doing my best to make sure the substance dissolves. It doesn't matter if the beer suddenly looks a little cloudy since he'll never see it.

I take one of the hardcover books from the closet and turn it over. It's the latest Stephen King novel. My mom buys books like this for us to read when she can. I get to go first, mostly because it takes her longer to finish. Unlike me, she doesn't have a lot of free time to spend reading. We keep the books hidden in my closet since my father doesn't approve of such frivolous purchases, insisting they're a waste of money. I've never seen him taking the time to read anything. The idea of catching him curled up with a book on the couch is absurd. It'd be like staring into the sky and catching sight of two moons. He gets irritated whenever we talk about our favorite books, so we try not to in his presence. Sometimes, I think he hates anything that makes us happy.

After sliding the dust jacket off and setting it aside, I place the book on the floor in the corner of the alcove. Here, no one can see it from the doorway. I pour some pills on the book and start crushing them with the smooth rock I found in the creek bed. It's the perfect size for the job—not *too* large to be cumbersome, though big enough to do the job. I'm able to quietly grind the pills down and sweep the rocky dust into the sandwich bag. Once I've crushed ten more pills and added them to my supply, I blow the dust off the rock, I wipe the book clean and put it away, and I seal the bag, shoving it under my pillow so I can easily retrieve it when the time is right.

Now, I wait.

Most of my life is spent waiting, watching, and listening for signs of what might be coming next. Always being on guard gets exhausting.

In the meantime...in the meantime, what? I turn to the blank pages of my notebook and start jotting down whatever comes to mind—

In the meantime.

In the *mean* time, I prove that I am crafty, I prove that I am cruel. Or, at least I can be. I will be. This time, when it counts the most, I will show no mercy.

In the *me* time, I suddenly have doubts. I stare at my hands, wondering if they're capable of doing what I need them to do. They've taken me this far, but is it far enough? Here I am, alone with these thoughts and notions, these plans and solutions. Here I am, alone, counting down the seconds, minutes, hours until I know the time is right. Here I am, hoping there's enough time. To get through this, to survive. But is the time I need even mine? Like everything else, I fear it belongs to him too. Time itself. His schedule, his rules, his everything.

Nothing else matters.

I slam my notebook shut and throw it across the room, tired of trying to figure out a riddle that can't be solved. Glancing down, I catch sight of a large oval bruise on my inner arm, right across my bicep. It's different from the others, the ones that have mostly faded. I can't remember where all these bruises come from. They start as deep, dark stains that slowly turn pale and sallow, fading until nothing's left. My mother says I'm clumsy, always tripping over something. My father—he doesn't say anything about them at all.

I bring my arm closer to my face, discovering that the dark oval mark fits the shape of my mouth. Now I remember—first there were bite marks, then the bruise. It was something I had to do. An irresistible urge. Like so many other things, it wasn't a decision I made. It just happened. I put my mouth to my arm and bit down hard, so hard it should have hurt more. With my own teeth, I nearly broke the skin, but I had to do it to keep the scream inside from finding its way out. There was a deeper pain, one that's always there. To forget that other pain, I bit down as hard as I could. Biting is better than screaming, and it worked. For a while, it worked.

Other bruises come and go, but this one I will remember.

A sudden movement at the far end of the house sends vibrations across the floor and through the walls—something rises, emerging from the dark. I feel unsteady and lightheaded, like an earthquake has shaken me loose, but I tell myself we don't get earthquakes here in the mountains, that we are safe from that, at least. But then I remember that my father *is* an earthquake. He's the disaster waiting to destroy us all.

It's him moving at the far end of the house, making his way to the kitchen. This could be it, the moment I've been waiting for. I snap out of it, breaking through the cloud that threatens to keep me in the dark. I look at the bruise one last time and jump into action. The bag of pills—my weapon of choice—is in my hand, is in my pocket. Carefully, I rise, making sure the mattress doesn't squeak. I'm in control again, *me*. This is my opportunity to change the course of our lives once and for all. I can't keep waiting for the wind to blow in a different direction. So far, these winds have done nothing but push us closer to the edge.

At the door, I pause long enough to listen carefully. His boots thump across the linoleum floor of the kitchen. For a few moments, there is silence, but then the sound of his steps returns as he heads back to the living room. The recliner groans like something dying as he falls into its musty embrace. While crossing to the bathroom, I casually glance down the hallway to see he's poured himself a cup of whiskey. I know it's whiskey because of the Styrofoam cup. He only uses those when he's drinking the hard stuff. He once kept the same dirty, white Styrofoam cup in the cabinet beside his booze for nearly a week. It started breaking down, crumbling from the alcohol. I don't know why he doesn't drink whiskey from a glass that can be washed regularly if he wants to use the same one. It's yet another thing about him I'll never understand.

Inside the bathroom, I shut the door and allow myself a little smile. I have a good feeling about this. I don't really need to pee but go through the motions anyway to make my trip to the bathroom more believable. With the tip of my foot, I lift the toilet seat and wait for what I feel is the appropriate amount of time it would take to empty my bladder before easing it back down and flushing. While washing up at the sink, I'm caught off guard by the sight of myself in the mirror. My face is pale, my eyes are gleaming with an excited fervor. For a moment, it's like someone else is standing before me, gazing out. Someone older, someone taller. Someone with similar features but who's so unlike me it sends a chill up my spine. Quickly, I bend down to splash water across my face. When I return my gaze to the mirror, whatever I saw is gone, but I can still feel its presence, waiting to reveal something I don't want to see.

I dry my face and close my eyes, focusing on what this is all about. The mission, the task. I must decide where to keep watch—the kitchen, the living room, or my bedroom? My bedroom is the obvious choice. I don't want to get too close to the target. Not yet. A flicker of doubt in my abilities to complete this gnaws at me. But I am stealthy in my moves, I have practiced the necessary steps to accomplish my goals. I can do this. In my bedroom, I can stay out of sight until the time is right. The swell of confidence returns. Without looking in the mirror again, I exit the bathroom and return to my bedroom, leaving the door wide open this time. Here, I'll wait—however long it takes.

And it doesn't take long. The sound of the recliner creaking when he gets up is a long, lonesome sigh of relief. His boots march my way, pounding across the living room and down the hall as he makes his way to the bathroom. I jump into action, armed with my bag of white powder. Keeping my ears perked and my eyes trained on the hallway, I dump about a third of the contents into his drink and quickly stir it with my finger. I panic for a moment, worried I've put too much in at one time to go unnoticed, but there's nothing I can do about it now. Slipping the bag back into my pocket, I rush to the kitchen and hear the bathroom door opening just as I reach the sink. I scrub my hands with soap to rinse the smell of whiskey away. I can't stand its strong, sharp odor. I can't stand anything about the rich, amber liquid since whiskey days are the worst

Just as he returns to his recliner, I freeze, holding my breath. Behind me, I can hear him leaning forward to grab his cup, pausing for what feels like an eternity before taking a sip. Eventually, he sets the cup down again—I don't hear it, exactly, but I can feel it happening. I wait, I listen. When I hear the creaking of the recliner as he settles in, I'm finally able to breathe again. He has no idea what I've done! My plan is working. I pour myself a glass of water and drink it down in one long gulp.

I wonder how many more cups of whiskey he'll have, how many more trips to the bathroom he'll take, and how many more chances I'll get to finish the job. Over the course of a typical whiskey day, he has at least three or four cups, leisurely drinking them as the late afternoon turns to night. He often mixes in a beer or two as well, going back and forth between that and his drink of choice. The more he has, and the quicker he throws them back, the better chance I have of making this work. It's an odd feeling, hoping he drinks more and quicker since I've come to dread his whiskey days so much. But today is different.

Waiting for the next step, I can't help but feel impatient. Just as I'm about to leave the kitchen to return to my post in the bedroom, I hear his recliner squeaking again. He's getting up, he's coming my way. We pass each other, predator and prey—I breathe in his musky scent. Near the sink, he's retrieving a glass, and in a split second, I decide to act, though I know it's risky. As he pours himself some water, I pull my bag out and dump more powder into his drink, quickly stirring it around with my finger. I'm quick but not quick enough—just as I'm turning away from what I've done, he's suddenly before me, staring down with cold, dark eyes.

"What are you doing?" he asks.

Surprisingly, I answer at once, "My friend Bobby says his dad always drinks beer after liquor, to like chase it. Is that what you do?"

He narrows his eyes, regarding me suspiciously. If he uncovers the truth, I might be the one who dies tonight. But then, his face softens, and I know I'm ok. "Hmm," he grunts. "Ever' now and then, I reckon."

I shrug and dart back to the kitchen, thinking about how Bobby doesn't even exist. I'm not sure where I came up with that. It'd be nice to have a friend named Bobby, though. It'd be nice to have a friend.

I shake it off—the loneliness—and focus on what a good job I'm doing. Not only have I managed to sneak more powder into his drink, but I've planted a seed in his mind making him think about how refreshing a nice cold beer would taste right about now. He'll be cracking one open any minute, I'm sure.

"Hey," he calls out, "bring me a beer then."

Alright, sure, I think, smiling like a killer. *Anything you want.*

In no particular rush, I open the fridge, I pull out a cold can from the back, and I bring it to him, all while keeping my mask of indifference carefully in place. My satisfied smile is now on the inside, bright and wide. I turn away and head back to my room, listening to the hiss of his beer popping open.

As the evening wears on, he takes two more bathroom breaks, allowing me plenty of time to sneak in two more doses of white sleeping dust. The last one almost finishes the bag. In my covert maneuvering, pretending I need a snack or more water from the kitchen, I peer over at him, taking note of his increasingly drowsy eyes. He's already having a hard time keeping them open, and his breathing has slowed, more so with each passing moment.

Who's in trouble now?

We'll say he got drunk like he always gets drunk, and he might have taken some pills. Too many pills. Really, we can't say for sure. We can't even say what kind of pills he takes. We're not aware of everything he does. There are things he wouldn't want us to know about, after all. That's true for anyone. Maybe it was suicide. He's always in a bad mood. Or, it could have been an accident. Maybe he didn't mean to take so many pills but lost count in his desperate need to get a good night of sleep. Drunk people make mistakes. They do stupid things all the time. They're capable of doing awful, destructive things that hurt themselves as much as they hurt those around them.

We don't have to say anything at all. Later, when this is all over, we can say we found him unresponsive, unable to wake him. His body stiff, his skin cold and rubbery, we don't know what happened. No one knows the truth but me, and I can keep my mouth shut. I've spent a lifetime learning how to stay quiet.

For now, he's still with us, but I can tell the pills are working. He starts to get up but immediately falls back, reaching a hand up to his head, his eyes, dizzy and confused; with great effort, he tries again, making it this time, though he's so unsteady on his feet he has to close his eyes and concentrate all his energy on remaining upright. Hunching over, he licks his lips, he runs his tongue over his teeth, trying to wet his parched mouth. Slowly, he looks around the room, which must be shifting out of focus by now. He mumbles a single word I can't quite understand; he tries again, just barely getting it out: *water.* He wants water. My sad, pathetic, dying dad, desperate for a drink of water to quench the unrelenting thirst he can't quite comprehend. His mouth, so fuzzy and dry, his head filled with a fog that thickens more as the mix of pills and alcohol take full effect. He takes a step towards the kitchen but seems to be having a hard time making his body do what he wants it to do. Changing course, he wobbles over to the couch, collapsing as his body gives out. The television drones on, though I doubt he can hear it—I doubt he can hear much of anything now, not with his senses beginning to fail. He shifts around uneasily, just barely managing to throw his arm over his face, sinking into the darkness. Accepting it because he has no choice. I can almost hear the sound of his cold black heart beating slower, and slower, and slower.

I watch his every move from the doorway of my bedroom, unafraid of him catching me. Unafraid of all the usual things, I watch him fall into a sleep that won't end. For the very first time, I feel completely unafraid.

I slip into the living room, turn the television off, and sit on the floor, crossing my legs to get more comfortable. All of this will be over soon.

—CAMERON L. MITCHELL (he/him)
Excerpt from The Last Way (forthcoming, Querencia Press 2025)

The sound of their voices and laughter echoed in that bare wooden house. His father had said something familiar to Mr. Frothingham as they arrived, like, "The sun is over the yardarm, so it must be time for a cocktail." They would be busy talking and getting louder for a quite a while.

He walked out along the same white sand that had led them there. The path from the front door led to the dirt-sand road, which ran back downhill toward the ferry dock, or uphill to his left. He thought he saw a man on a bicycle in the distance, traveling uphill. As his eyes followed the road, he saw the top half of the man descending over the horizon, as if he were being lowered into the space beyond. What else could there be across this mostly barren landscape except more of the same small, white houses that came up this way from the village, set here and there along this furrowed road?

He started walking in the man's direction, conscious that the sun also hung there, just about touching the edge of the hill. He felt the heat coming across the sand, low down like someone aiming a big flashlight that burned his knees as he walked. He was aware that he was counting his steps and had just reached 215 when he didn't want to count anymore. The island was silent except for faint cries of seagulls that he couldn't see and the rhythmic, crisping sound of his sneakers in the sand. He studied the irregular track of the bicycle and the grooves it left. Whoever was riding it managed to make the back tire follow the front to leave one neat groove, mostly. He knew this meant the man was riding fast enough to keep it steady and straight. Maybe he had a long way to go or was in a hurry. Or maybe he had come this way many times and knew the line to follow.

As the boy came to the top of the rise, more of the island came into view, falling away to the ocean bay that now glared across the late afternoon in a way that hurt his eyes. The road had tufts of grass in the middle—there must've been cars here once upon a time, or maybe farm wagons. But he could see no signs of large animal feet to pull a wagon, so that made no sense. The path of the bicycle tire was a shallow trench of firm sand that felt like a line he was meant to follow, just to see where it led. The island smelled of salt—and faintly of Christmas trees—and the line of the tire might have been a tiny stream flowing empty down this gradual hill and bending in that afternoon light towards the ocean.

A small cluster of buildings marked a turn in the road, or maybe it was some kind of crossing. It might be a house and a separate barn or a shed or two. He couldn't be sure and the hint of movement around the base of one building made him think of farm animals. What could live here? As the question came into his mind, he noticed the vegetation had changed on the long downhill slope off to his right, as if this side of the island, facing the afternoon sun and subject to the mild breeze coming up the hill toward him now, might give some advantage for grasses to grow.

A meadow now appeared to stretch along the road and extend down to what he recognized as a small farm, or at least a white house with a separate white barn. A line of fence encircled the meadow and embraced the small oval pond at the bottom of the hill. From behind him suddenly a large black bird darted over his right shoulder. Its erratic, beating movement against the sky made him jump before it shrank against the rim of pale green land below the buildings near the pond. He watched it pull up sharply to alight on the wire fence that started at the barn and ran around the pond across the bottom of the meadow. A crow, was that it? He could not think of any other black birds by name except the one in the poem by Edgar Allan Poe that he had memorized in third grade. Raven? Maybe a cormorant, the long-necked water bird his father had pointed out in the distance as they came in on the ferry earlier that afternoon. A cormorant had to make a quick dash on the water's surface, its webbed feet slapping loudly before take-off, his father said, because its wings had trouble shedding water. The bird on the fence didn't seem to have much of a neck. It settled itself into a concentrated black dot about the size of a baseball glove. Then it let out a sharp, angry sound that might've been the word "dark!" except birds can't talk. Well, parrots do. He noticed the sun had fallen further toward the horizon onto a mound of grey clouds that looked like fireplace ashes.

He had lost track of his own footsteps somehow, his steady progress down the road close enough to see the buildings in detail and to realize that this road must be their road. It crossed in front of the square, two-story, white house with black shutters and a large chimney in the center. His footsteps seemed to have a plan of their own, because as the road bent around the house, he found himself standing in a courtyard facing two open barn doors, a gloomy interior of dark posts and a heavily beamed ceiling within. He could hear a muffled sound from the barn that made him think of lots of little people with thin, persistent voices, all trying to say the word "ever" at the same time. Each time one of them said "ever," another would quickly chime in, then another. The sound of one became the sound of the next, and so on, into a nearly constant stream. "Ever-eh-ver- ever-eh-eh-ver."

"You curious?"

The old man's voice from the shadows just inside the barn entered him like a dart and made him jump back slightly, followed almost immediately by the man's angular face catching the light, his shoulders and chest in a maroon and grey checked shirt and dark blue overalls moving out from behind one post. He was unshaven and had a forceful, wiry build and bright grey eyes.

"Where'd you come from?" he asked.

The second question followed quickly on the first as the boy was still considering the word "curious." Yes, he guessed he was curious. Why else would he have walked this way, followed the road to its end, come around the house into the courtyard where he was suddenly aware that it belonged to strangers in a strange place?

What was the answer to the question, where had he come from? From up the road, from Mr. Frothingham's, or from a small dairy town in Massachusetts where barns like this usually meant farm animals inside?

"We have a barn like this," he said. He didn't mean a barn exactly like this. Theirs was a three-story barn built of heavy timbers, made for milking cows on the ground floor and storing hay in two levels above, with an empty silo at one end. It still smelled sweet. The barn had stood empty since his parents bought the property from the farmer who died. All they really needed was the house, but they got the barn and the old widow selling the place threw in all the rest of the land, about 140 acres, for nothing, his father said. He liked to tell that story and told it often.

"You a farmer then, too?" the man asked. He scrutinized the boy with a sidelong, squinty look, his face rumpled like a walnut shell. His upper lip suddenly drew his face up into a grimace that exposed his top teeth before settling back to normal, a flash of something the boy had not seen before. Maybe trying to clean his teeth or release tension from the bagged skin under his eyes.

The boy was not sure if this was a real question or a joke the man was making, so he waited. The man seemed to look through and past him to the road and said, after a pause, "You come a long way down here on your own."

This seemed not so much a statement as a question. Maybe the man was asking him again where he had come from or, maybe, what he was doing here? The boy knew he had no good reason for being here except he walked here somehow.

"The road comes down here," he said. This was not much of an answer, and he felt heat rise in his face. He noticed a bicycle leaning against the barn wall and raised his hand to point at it.

"That your bike?"

The man glanced at it.

"Elmira," he said. "I get on her when I need to and she takes me wherever I want to go. Though not fast. You got one?"

The boy nodded. He pictured the red, Robin Hood three-speed he inherited from his older sister the year before and his first efforts to drive it on the pot-holed road uphill from their house between empty pastures. His head filled with too many ideas and images all at once.

"Yessir," he said.

"Yessir?!" repeated the man. "Raised respectful we were, en?"

The boy did not know what to make of that question either. It reminded him of a day he saw his cousin being whipped by his uncle, who kept demanding, "Do you know why you are being whipped?", "Yessir" his cousin finally replied through his tears, and the beating stopped.

In this moment the boy did not know why the word came to him and came out so quickly as his own.

"Yessir," he said again, a little louder. "Do you have animals n your barn?"

"Animals in my barn? Sure I got animals. I got feed. I got tools, tractor parts, more mice 'en you can shake a stick at. Sheep, mostly."

His words drew his right hand up to his face to scrub his forehead and squeeze his cheeks into his nose and pull his mouth down towards his chin, all in one motion. Then he flexed his jaw wide open, and pulled his upper lip back again over his top teeth as if to scrape them clean. This seemed to give him new energy. He gestured back into the barn.

"C'mon, I'll show you my little herd. Just in for the night."

Here the boy knew something—or did he sense it, and not knowing what sensing was, exactly, or how to interpret it, felt something come into his body, a hollow sensation along the bones in his forearms. He was about to cross a line, like from the road to the courtyard, or from the courtyard to inside the barn. He did want to see the sheep and maybe a tractor or two. Still, this was a strange place and where he was exactly, and how he got here, were getting mixed up with what he should say or do next.

"You said you got a barn? You look like you might know your way around a barn." the man said, his bright grey eyes fixing on the boy's chest. "How old are you, boy?"

"Going on 11," he said. "We have a barn that used to be for cows but we don't use it for that anymore."

"What do your folks do, then?"

"My father goes to an office in the city and my mother stays home and cooks and cleans the house," he said.

"Office is clean work if you can get it," the man said. "Me, I like to be outside. And the less people the better, if you know what I mean. C'mon this way."

He turned abruptly and stepped into the barn to follow the outside wall into the shadows. The boy felt himself drawn along behind as if on some kind of string, the checked shirt and overalls and rubber boots pulling him down this corridor that smelled intensely of hay and manure. The air in the barn was thick and hot on his skin, like the breath of too many animals in a small space. He saw some tools on the wall—a crosscut saw, a scythe, two antique rakes, a pickaxe, and a large pincer-like tool he knew was for digging holes. He recognized these from all the tools left behind in their barn by the farmer who died and whose widow, his mother explained one night at dinner, wanted nothing to do with any of it anymore. This barn was longer than he expected, built on the downhill so he suddenly came to six tall steps, which he counted down to a lower dirt floor. He could hear faint bleating as the man reached a sliding door and prepared to pull it open.

"All you been through is for tools and storage and such. Back here the animals come in to feed and sleep.," the man said. "Daytime they go out to the field and the pond. You're not afraid of sheep, are you?" The man followed this with his little bark of a laugh.

The boy heard the question as a challenge—or a dare. What kind of boy would he be if he was afraid of a few sheep?

"No sir," he said emphatically and looked through the open door into another darkening space. This had a low roof sloping down over a set of small pens. They were like square boxes of wooden gates on either side of a narrow central corridor to the far opening. There, another big door stood open toward the pond. It took several moments for these shapes to come clear as the boy's eyes adjusted to the light, illuminated by a single, bare, overhead bulb dangling in the middle. He was aware of low, rounded greyish shapes moving in the pens and the sound of hay being rustled around. He listened intently for the sound of bleating but for some reason they had all fallen silent.

The man had stopped halfway down the corridor to look back at him, the glare from the bulb bright on his forehead. The boy felt himself being examined as if something more were expected of him now, some question he should ask or something he should say about coming into a stranger's barn. Was it curiosity that led him there? Where did curiosity come from? This question caused a swirly sensation in his head as if his mind was turning around to see things differently. If his mother were here, she would tell him to be polite and stand up straight and look at the man directly. He tried to do this now, although he felt a certain force coming from the man at this distance of about three bicycle lengths.

What was that feeling in the air? Or was it the gathering darkness, or maybe the warmth that spread out from the clusters of huddled sheep he could now faintly make out, one group in each pen, all silently chewing with sideways jaw movements? He felt himself embraced or surrounded, or in a blanket, perhaps. In the nearest pen to the right, one light brown face among darker ones looked out at him from down low between the boards. Its dark eyes fixed on him kindly, its small jaws working back and forth, bringing stray shoots of hay into its charcoal mouth, two eyes like shiny black buttons concentrating on him. He was aware of being watched as he was watching, not just the sheep but the man, who stood in the narrow corridor, one elbow cocked onto each of the two railings that ran between the pens. Outlined against the far exit, he looked like a scarecrow, motionless but meaning something with his attitude.

"You're wondering how many sheep I got," said the man. "I can see you are the curious type."

"Yes," the boy said. "I was wondering." He had not been wondering that before but now he was. He could do the math in his head that four or five sheep in each of four pens would mean 16 or 20. He couldn't imagine any more than that in this space.

"Thirty-six, to be exact," said the man. "We had close to a hunnert when my old man ran them in the early days of this island. Everyone here ate our lamb and we carded our wool and spun it and the women knitted and we used to joke that people hereabouts wear our sheep inside and out."

He shrugged for emphasis. Another small bark of a laugh pulled his face into a twisted expression that closed his eyes for a moment. The boy stared at the man's forehead where the light of the overhead bulb concentrated into a brilliant yellow spot. Then the man stepped back into the shadows and made a gesture for the boy to follow. He stepped forward between the pens, conscious of the heat and odor coming off the animals on both sides, aware that they were watching him move into the corridor between them.

"Come around this end and let me introduce you to Elsa," said the man. "That she's our prize ewe won't surprise *you*."

Another half-bark came that might have been the man's laugh and the boy realized he'd made a joke in the way the words sounded the same but meant something different. He didn't respond, watching the sheep watch him. The man stood now at the end holding a smaller gateway open to the last pen.

"You can pet Elsa in here and feel how deep her wool goes," he said.

The boy saw something in his face when he said it, or maybe it was his eyes, the way the light seemed to concentrate in the grey around two dark pinpoint pupils and come toward him like twin arrows converging on his face and neck and chest, like lines drawn with a hot pen that burned ever so slightly, he could feel heat rising from his stomach to his chest and neck and face as if someone had switched something on, the burner under a pot of water on the stove, how bubbles collect on the side and break away one by one to rise to the surface, he felt something rising in him because of the man's eyes and the way they crisscrossed on him now.

He stepped into the pen where Elsa stood alone, chewing her own mouthful of hay. He reached down to press his fingers deep into her coat, amazed to feel the wool stretch down beyond the length of his fingers as if she had no body at all.

"I don't know where you came from, but you appear as fine an all-American boy as a man could ever hope to see down this way," the man added.

The boy felt the compliment as a new feeling he did not have a name for, an odd mixture of pleasure and discomfort. He felt a little like afraid but not quite afraid because he was curious about the sounds and smell of the sheep and how old was Elsa and why the air tasted different from the barn air he knew at home or at the neighbor's further down Route 113, a barn so full of Holsteins the summer air got sharp in your throat to breathe the steam off the manure pile that blew back into the barn.

The air here had a softer, cooler feeling, a scent of vegetation mixed with wool. He couldn't put words on this either. Too many ideas and sensations converged in his head at once and the man's voice was piling on top. It carried the tone of a friend who had an idea maybe of something to do and he was about to reveal it.

"I was just walking,' the boy explained, as much to himself as to the man. "Sometimes I just like to walk to see where I end up."

He was thinking more about his farm, no longer home to farm animals but a sprawling set of pastures divided by stone walls and ending at pine forests that bounded the property to the north and east. He could wander wherever he wanted though he usually got a little afraid before he reached the end of the property in any direction. He liked to walk up behind the barn through the orchards to the open hayfield beyond the first stone wall and cross that to the next wall, and into another pasture, often filled with the neighbor's cows, that stretched to yet another. It ended their property to the north at another stone wall at the edge of the woods. He didn't like to go beyond that for reasons he could not describe. A feeling stopped him at the edge and he always turned back for home at that point.

"I didn't know anyone lived here," he said.

"Yes, well, not just anyone lives here," said the man, letting out a chuckle that sounded like small stones falling into a metal bucket. "Someone lives here who has lived here his whole life and that would be me. And I can't rightly recall a visitor who was anything like you. You have a special ability that sets you apart, else you wouldn't have got here on your own."

When the man said, "got here on your own," the boy thought about his own—his own way and his own idea to walk up the road, and some things that were not his own, too, like coming to this island in the first place and spending the night so his parents could drink with the Frothinghams. They all seemed very far away from the space around him and the man's face now obscure, his face so dimly lit as to resemble a wooden mask. It gave the boy an odd feeling of being contained and surrounded, first by the barn and then by the encroaching darkness and now by the sound of the man's voice and the feeling of him nearby, staring, his face still working around his mouth and lips, uncovering and covering his teeth in a nervous way, like biting his fingernails, only different. Maybe something about a barn full of sheep makes your mouth go dry. His mouth felt funny, it was becoming difficult to swallow his own spit, which suddenly he had less of than normal.

"I have something to show you," the man said, gesturing toward the far end of the barn. "Come down there with me for a moment."

He held down his left hand with his fingers apart and the boy saw himself reach for it, even as something—he could not say what it was—tried to hold him back. He felt the man's rough hand encircle his and draw him toward the far shadows of the barn to see what the thing might be. Maybe a tractor.

The sheep had gone totally quiet. He was aware of them moving around on the hay. He could almost feel the silence around them in the fragrance of the hay and the wool, and the man close by with eyes on him, and suddenly now, the man's hands were on his shoulders holding him upright against the side of the stall with a broken humming sound coming out of the man that might have had breath in it or a sound of pushing air and the boy felt his own breathing stop, held in his chest, stuck between trying to breathe out and breathe in, a wad of air in his chest and the sensation of pressure from the man's body leaning against his against the stall and trembling, and the man saying, "All right now, all right, easy now," and the boy was aware of freezing or being frozen there upright, the man's hard body leaning into him and pressing harder until a convulsion of some kind trembled through the man and he made a sound like a cow lowing in a faraway pasture, like when they want to come home, a kind of groan with a note in it, the boy knew this from the neighbor's cows but he had never heard it come out of a man like that, or anyone. And just then he felt something hot on his leg that might have been oil or fat from a pan but couldn't possibly be. He couldn't see where it came from and the man was stepping back away from him now and fumbling with his overalls and turning away saying, "Just a minute, just a minute here," and the boy heard the man getting angry in talking to himself, he could not tell exactly what was happening in the dim light of the pen as the man reached back to him with a handkerchief or something to wipe the oil off his leg.

"Sorry, so sorry—you're a perfect lad," the man said, "We've got to get you on your way, wouldn't you say now?" The words rushed out to pile up on themselves in the boy's mind.

Something in the barn itself had changed; the air had a new quality that wasn't there before they came down toward the back where the shadows made it so hard to see what the man was doing. The boy felt an intense urgency to get back to the front of the barn and outside. He wasn't sure if this was his idea or the farmer's, who was making faint sounds like someone talking to himself without wanting anyone else to hear or understand what he was saying. This set off some of the sheep close by, a conversation springing up amongst them and now spreading through the barn, one bleat nearby and another at a little distance, "*ever-ever- rah-ever-eh-eh-eh.*" The boy felt these notes as well as heard them, passed around among the sheep like a message about the farmer and him. Maybe they were telling him to go back to wherever he came from or they were settling down to sleep and didn't want him around anymore or they knew something he needed to know and were trying to tell him as best they could.

"Yessir, I have to go back now," he said. The words came out in a smaller voice than he was used to hearing in his head. They struggled to get out of his dry lips and this new, smaller version of himself. He was conscious of moving in some kind of lockstep with the farmer, who came towards him as he stepped back. He could feel the space between them closing again and he worked to enlarge it as he retreated faster up the channel between the pens toward the front of the barn where he had come in.

"Where you off to now?" the farmer said.

The boy heard it not so much as a question about where he was going but about whether he would go, or would he go now, or later? Maybe he wouldn't go at all, but stay? He had never meant to stay. Coming down here was more like an accident. This new question or whatever it was exactly threw a chill into him that he had never felt.

"Going back to the F—" he started to explain. Something in him stopped the name from coming out and he searched for another word that started with F that would not give away his destination or the people who were the reason he was on the island in the first place. "The front—of the road," he said.

This was all happening so fast, this pressure building within him to get out of the barn, feeling pulled backwards and also pushed by the feeling of the farmer close behind him as he approached the barn opening. Then, with the courtyard suddenly in view but barely lit by the remnants of the day and the beginning of the night, he broke into a run toward the space and was not sure if the sounds behind him were the sounds of a man trying to overtake him or maybe the faint echoes of his own steps across the sandy gravel as he fled.

Everything now had gone from pale to nearly dark or darkly pale, the way the woods go at the edge of the field when night falls, when so many trees turn to one in the darkness coming on and you realize that soon you will not be able to see one thing from another or know just where you are. He ran with what might have been small wings—he was not aware of touching the ground as much as passing over it, though he could hear the sounds of his sneakers on the sand on the right edge of the roadway, he was feeling his way with his feet and for a reason he could not fathom he pictured the farmer bent over the handlebars of Elmira coming after him. Those tires would make no sound in the sand as they came up behind him and this idea filled his chest to crowd out all the air he was trying to gulp down as he ran.

He came up the first long incline to the top of the hill and suddenly outran his own feet. He felt himself take off headfirst into the dark and come down almost as quickly on all fours, hands and knees hitting the sand at the same moment, like a dog, as he pictured himself, when his chin struck the ground with a burning in his hands and knees at almost the same time. The specter of the farmer on his bicycle propelled him up again and he did not dare look back for fear of making fear come true. Maybe if he did not look back the farmer could not be there.

Why would he come after him? Something had happened in the barn between them. The boy was not sure what he had done that was wrong or caused the farmer to act so strangely, but he knew that he had done something he shouldn't have done, he had no business being there and should never speak of it ever, even if someone asked.

Where had he gone? What had he been doing? The questions wheeled in his mind like crows or cormorants in midair and still he ran. He did not know his body could propel him like this even as he felt he might explode or be snatched up from behind and held to account for the thing that had just happened. And just then he saw a faint figure on the road approaching uphill, coming toward him with a flashlight, and the shadow of the dark figure behind the blade of the light and the lighter sand of the roadway was the familiar shape of his father, coming to find him.

—ERIC BEST (he/him)

NONFICTION

A Month After

A few weeks after your mother dies you will stand in the middle of your room. You will clench the hospital bag holding her belongings. The ground will feel too hard, and your clothes will feel too tight. You will ask yourself how you let this happen.

You will turn off the lights in the room so you can see better. There will be nothing to see except a room littered with empty water bottles, three half empty bowls of soup you tried and failed to eat this weekend, and clothes you couldn't bring yourself to pick up. You will walk past your journal. You will have already tried to write, but nothing will come to mind until you go back to college—a week later.

Your knife will stay in its hiding place. All you will think about is the time your mother saw your cuts and slapped you. She told you, "Never do that shit again." You will laugh bitterly at the thought of using the knife. Feeling envious of the time when you felt it helped.

When you stop screaming, you will stub your toe trying to get to your bed in the dark. The tears will come and you will wonder if they will ever stop.

Two days before you left for your first year of college your mother dragged you to Target. She told you what to buy and you argued with her. You will wish you bought that big expensive tool box, a month after she dies, when you are putting together furniture at college. Your mother will prove herself to always be right, and your brother will ask why furniture makes you cry.

You will spend money you don't have on things you should've gotten when you first went to college. You will feel guilty for the money you spend on Etsy and Amazon, but you will keep scrolling. You will buy three books that you will only read ten pages of all together, a pack of post-it notes that fall off as soon as they are placed, and you will buy a thin flower shaped pillow for your chair. When the pillow on your bed starts to itch from the dirt and follicles from weeks of being unwashed, you will use the thin pillow as your only pillow.

Your grandmother will buy you a white bed sheet. Your bed sheet had a small rip before your mother died, and you never changed it after she went. The rip will have grown so large that, in the mornings, you wake up with your legs inside of it touching the urine stained mattress beneath.

She will say, "It's unacceptable."

You will not reply, you will look down at the ground.

She'll sigh and softly tell you, "Let me know before it gets this bad again."

You do not respond, instead you lie down on the first clean sheet you've slept on in a while. When she leaves, you will wonder if things *have* gotten bad. Then you will wonder if she was still talking about the sheet.

A month after your mother dies, you will be excited for college. You will fantasize about escaping your chaotic emotion ridden house, but then, on your first day back at college, you will experience homesickness for the first time and be unable to stop crying.

Your partner will ask, "Are you okay?"

And all you'll be able to get out through the sobs is, "I will be."

After you run out of tears you will hug your dog and sleep on the floor, clutching the blanket your mom died in. You will do it again and again for the next week but you won't cry.

Your back hurts and you're exhausted until your partner starts picking you up off the floor and putting you on the bed. You will fight to sleep on the floor. You won't know why, but you will fight anyway. Your exhaustion will ensure you lose. Eventually, on the fourth night, you willingly sleep in the bed, and when you do, you cry and your partner holds you to sleep.

Later that same week when your therapist asks, "How are you doing?"

All you will say is, "I'm alive." because it's true and you don't want to worry anyone.

When your friends talk about things other than your mother's death, you will get quiet.

Your chest will tighten with anger when they rant about class as they always do, and you will try to hold back tears when you think about how your mother is dead and nothing has changed here except you. When you go back to your dorm after seeing them you will ask yourself, "Was I too boring?"

A month after your mother dies you will sit down and write a story for class. You will try to write about something other than your grief. You will not be able to. So you will write about your mother.

146

—GRAY DAWSON (he/him)

And I found myself here again, on your bed, on Saturday, 2 p.m., it's our routine checkup. We only meet on Saturdays, early afternoon, your hand on my thigh. My body is tense, I don't want to lean on you too dependently, only barely, only for us to pretend.

It did not take any courage to admit I didn't love you to Michelle, and she already knew before I told her. I did not tell her I wanted you to love me, but maybe she already knew that as well. I'm a selfish bastard—I've always wanted to be loved, but only quietly. I ran when it became overbearing; begged when I felt the love fading away. Ironically, I'm scared to find out if there is a reason for this tendency, I can only hope this is how I have always been. I'm scared to hear this is a result of feeling undesirable when I was younger. I don't think I was. I am terrified I was, I haven't been me since I was younger, any love now is pointless. I tell myself this is the most humane response, and I pray I am correct. Everyone is ike me. Everyone is me, this is only a common archetype.

When you pull yourself off me, I want you to tell me you love me, even if you don't mean it. Even if all you want is my body below yours. My breath is palpable and raw. I will not love you. I will write stories about you. I will create you and hate you and you will leave and I will be okay. You have loved me, and it will pass.

No.

At a pub on a Sunday night, I pulled a girl in, or maybe she, me—and I could taste her lipstick and vodka-cran, her eyes lidded, her breasts pushed into mine. People are screaming around us, I remember the peanut butter cookies I had at the pregame, and I am terrified she's allergic like you. The pub tiles are wet, so I can slip into her, her into people, people into us—my feet are still cold, we waited in line thirty minutes, in -10 degrees, to get in, and she's holding my waist, no it's not her—and she pulls away, or maybe she was never there at all. Laughing with her friends. Smudges the lines of her lips. They're still perfectly drawn. She doesn't look back—I need a shot.

No.

And I'm at the bar counter, my friends are dancing. I recognize their heads, four brunettes, three blondes, I pull out my phone, the glare is blinding, only for a second. Bullet chess. Here, sex is a god. We breathe it in, gateway drug, it did not smell like this on your bed; we were only playing.

I win all my games, my elo peaked, "You spent three point five hours on Chess" stupid screen time. My fingers are jittery, and my lips are bruised. My jacket smells like cheap beer, laced with the saccharine of grenadine. I called you that night, forty-one seconds outgoing.

What do you want from me. Do you want me to tell you I love you too? Cry and beg and plead when you leave, kiss and suck your body like it's coated with propofol—I'm an insomniac, I haven't slept properly in 14 months. I'm not on any sleep medication. Sometimes, I take melatonin and pretend. I bought these gummies off Amazon for 30.99. They taste like cherries, and stick on your teeth like algae on rock, sweet with an ugly aftertaste, and I lie in bed, eyes closed. Sometimes, I forget how to breathe, and I have to teach myself again. It doesn't come naturally in the beginning, and I spend hours on end, eyes closed, gummy melting on my teeth—in and out. In and out. In and out.

No.

I do like you. I confessed to you at a house party on the 25th. I blame it on the alcohol, but I had it planned out sober, intoxication is my favorite scapegoat recently, that and inherent humanity. But I hate your scarf, your vernacular on texts. Your peanut allergy. Your gentle-parent smile. Your aversion towards capitalization. Your ankle-length skinny jeans, your audacity and shamelessness. Your—you know I am immature and young and despicable and I hate myself and I can never sleep. I cut off caffeine but my heart is still rabid at 4 a.m., and when I drink I am a narcissistic people-pleaser. The sun rises now, almost comical, like a lucky-charm cereal box cut-out. It's orange and cancerous. There's a text from you. "hope u got back home safe."

I need to get off the sofa. My boots are wet. My feet are cold. Someone waterlogged my phone last night. It refuses to charge. I'll put it in rice later. I think I saw that on Instagram. You've liked my post. Seven new follow requests. I'll need to block them. 278 blocked profiles. 285 blocked profiles.

I called you drunk at the pub. Travis Scott's Fein. No, he's just my friend. I should hang up. You sleep early. We should do a shot. I never tried a blowjob before, is it good? I heard it tastes like chocolate milk.

—JUHEON RHEE (she/her)

At the start of summer, your girlfriend's mother gives you a bag of figs.

You don't think she knows that she's "your girlfriend's mother" yet. You've only been dating her daughter for a few weeks, and nothing about the relationship was clear. You confessed your feelings to her daughter in May, after she pointed her finger at you, almost accusatory, and declared that you "made her nervous."

You haven't asked her to be your girlfriend yet, but in three months you will. You'll be in a Taco Bell parking lot, and it will be your turn to be nervous. It will be dark and you'll be grateful for it because it will hide how red your face is. And even though, by then, you already know that her answer is *yes,* the act of asking will be enough to make your heartbeat flutter.

But you will have had a summer between you before you do.

Your girlfriend was careful to warn you in advance to accept all gifts given—don't say *no* when you mean *yes,* and only say *thank you*, even if you wanted to say *no* before it. *It's cultural*, she said, *a sign of affection*. So, you know you have no choice but to accept the Old Navy bag her mother hands you, filled with hand-picked figs from the tree in her backyard.

Your girlfriend is so proud—you can tell—that you're worthy to receive such a present. For her sake, you'll try to ignore the panic rising inside you.

Maybe you'll make a jam, you tell her mother.

"Bite into one now," her mother insists, "they're so sweet."

But you know you can't. All you can think about is what's inside.

Your therapist knows you're weird about food—that some days you wake up and fully believe everything in the house is inedible. She knows that any kind of blemish, real or imagined, means that the whole thing is getting tossed. That whatever container it was in is getting washed twice. Once to get the mold you know is sticking to the microscopic pores of the tupperware. Then again, to actually get it clean.

Your therapist knows that you can't stand the thought of consuming something that is contaminated. You can't eat blue cheese because it gets its blue from mold—you've never dared to touch it. You can't drink cow's milk unless it was moved from the fridge to a glass then gulped down before it could rise one degree above 39°F.

You will remember how it felt to hold the figs in your hand—long after they were gone. Soft and round, the color of a bruise. They were so delicate, crushable in your palm like little bird hearts. Your therapist would probably understand why now, you can't bring yourself to bite the fruit.

When you ask your girlfriend's mom about the wasps, she laughs, dismissive. "They're long gone now," she says.

But not to you. Instead you'll claim you're just not hungry and thank her for the gift.

For the rest of the day, you carry the Old Navy bag with you around the city. You can't leave them in your car—the heat index was 104 and the black leather interior of your Honda could easily reach 115—but you wish you didn't have to look at them.

You don't know it yet, but you will spend the rest of that summer thinking about lesbianism and the Philippines. One of which you know well, and the other you'll grow to love. To your girlfriend, both were essential.

You will bond over words like *chisme* and *tsismis*, relaxing into her hand when you don't have to explain what the Spanish word for "gossip" is. How the English translation "to be a gossip" is nowhere near the power of the *chismosa*.

It will be a private, quiet victory when you're at an event together, months later, and you'll be the only non-Fillipina to get the accent right on someone's name. Abandoning the American bravado for flattening out sounds that should dance. You won't be able to show too much excitement when another two women joke about being a *bruja*—another shared translation between you two—or a *manananggal*. You recognized the latter from stories of folk beings your girlfriend shared.

For now, though, you avoid looking at the bag you left on your countertop. Nothing else at home the next day will seem edible either—taken over and burrowed into by imaginary creatures overnight.

It was a fact you stumbled upon a few years ago, that *ficus carica*—the common fig—relied on the female wasp for pollination. She buries inside the unripe fruit—losing her wings and antennae in the process—to lay her eggs inside. It becomes both her nursery and her grave, when the wasp dies. Her eggs hatch. Males and females mate. Then, wingless males die beside their mother, and the female wasps tunnel their way out. Flying away, fertilized, in search of their own fig.

You know that logically, this happens early on in the ripening process, that their insect bodies were broken down long ago. But to you, it will always be there at the center.

Your girlfriend finds the wasps and the fruit beautiful, and you don't tell her otherwise.

She is a poet, making a habit of stringing details together. Each image, a piece of popcorn she carefully pierces and slides onto a strand of garland. Once the garland is long enough, her poems wrap around you. Tying you up and making it difficult to breathe.

You will joke together about making art—how you each have a quota for writing one piece a year and then burning out. But you know she will break that pattern to write about the harvest. Her kitchen overflowing with figs, she will have no choice but to write an ode to the insect that died to create them. The poem will be beautiful, and you will reread it at least three times. Each time, you will be haunted by the fruit you left sitting on the counter.

Later that year you will joke about getting her to write another poem, for an all-time record of four. In return, she will send you a rough outline for the one she would write about your breasts:

Something something gay panic

Something something celestial bodies

Boobs and life and death, etc.

Then, you'll laugh and remember the face she made when you thumbed the button of your shirt.

You bring the figs with you to visit your friends, seven hours away. Three days before, you woke up angry at yourself for not thinking to put them in the fridge. You drove up with them in a cooler pack. Maybe you imagined the buzzing in your trunk, or maybe it was the thump of your own heart.

For two days, you help your friends move into a new apartment. You watch them, greedy, for what eight years of dating has turned them into. Everything belongs to each other, even their stories. They talk about coworkers, budgeting, and their grocery list for the week. They say they are jealous because unlike you, they've never lived alone. You never feel lonelier than when you're around them. How they each live like one half of a whole.

Exhausted, your friend goes to the fridge one night and asks you for a fig. They promised to make jam with you, but wanted a quick snack. You had already told them all of your stories—of your confessions and her mother's Old Navy bag.

You were so afraid, then, of everything. You had only been dating for a month and you asked yourself every question you could.

Your friend pulls a fig from the container you had put in the fridge. She's never had a fresh one before, but she stops and frowns. She shows her fiancé, and you can sense the white fluff before they even mention it. You wave a hand—you don't want to look—and they dump the gift from your girlfriend's mom in the trash. Tomorrow, you will take the tupperware home with you and you'll wash it twice. But tonight you lie under the covers and cry.

You won't tell your girlfriend what happened to them. You'll tell her you made that jam, but left the mason jars behind. Everything between you is new and in bloom and you're scared of making the wrong move—of saying *no* when you mean *yes*—and the figs are still in season.

You haven't even asked her to be your girlfriend yet.

Months later, long after the Taco Bell, the *chismis*, and her poetry, when temperatures start to graze the line between *cool* and *cold* and anything insectile dies away, you'll think again about the wasp. You'll begin to wonder if, for her, crawling back into the fruit felt like coming home.

Sitting in the shower in the dark, mirror fogging up from all the steam, you'll light a candle, and maybe play something nostalgic that strums from your phone. You'll shave your legs—realizing later that you missed a spot— and for the first time, you'll wonder what those figs might have tasted like if you had sunken in your teeth and taken a bite.

—HELEN PELUSO (she/her)

ABOUT THE CONTRIBUTORS

⁎ **Abbie Langmead** (she/they) is a Sapphic Jewish writer originally from Boston, MA and currently living in Dublin, Ireland. Their poetry has recently appeared in *North New England Review*, *BarBar*, *Trace Fossils Review*, and many others. Find them in those places, walking very confidently when she doesn't actually know where she's going, or hosting dinner parties in her apartment.

⁎ **Alina Kalontarov** (she/her) is a teacher of English literature and Humanities in New York City. Her work can be found in *Sky Island Journal*, *Scribeworth*, *Thimble Literary Magazine*, *Boats Against the Current*, *Overgrowth Press*, *Prosetrics*, *Wild Roof Journal*, *Last Leaves Magazine*, and *Words Apart: A Globe of Poetry*.

⁎ **Alix Perry** is a trans writer from the Pacific Northwest. Their work has been nominated for the *Best of the Net Anthology* and can be found in *The Shore*, *The B'K*, *beestung*, and elsewhere. *Tomatoes Beverly* is their debut poetry chapbook. Follow their work at alixperrywriting.com and @_alixperry_ on social media.

⁎ Maine native **Anastasia Walker** (she/her/hers) is a queer poet, essayist, and scholar living in Pittsburgh. Her first book of poetry, *The Girl Who Wasn't and Is*, was published in 2022. Her essays have appeared in several journals. She has also blogged on politics, social media, and trans/LGBTQ+ issues for both *Huffington Post* and *Medium*. She's a passionate amateur musicologist, and a lover of long walks and swimming in the ocean. Her blog: https://anastasiaswalker.blogspot.com/.

⁎ **A.S. Aubrey** is a psychotherapist/writer working with trauma, chronic illness and identity. Her work has been seen or is forthcoming in *The Poets Corner's Art & Ekphrastic Poetry exhibit*, *The Write Launch*, *Ipa'lante!*, *Cathexis Northwest Press*, *Hare's Paw*, *Voices/1922 Review*, *Libre*, *Journal X* and *The Bookends Review*. She currently lives in Los Angeles, where the urban sprawl inspires humor and existential angst.

⁎ **Benjamin Goluboff** is the author of *Ho Chi Minh: A Speculative Life in Verse* and *Biking Englewood: An Essay on the White Gaze*, both from Urban Farmhouse Press. Goluboff teaches at Lake Forest College. Some of his work can be read at https://www.lakeforest.edu/academics/faculty/goluboff

⁎ **Birch Wiley** is a transsexual poet living in New York. Birch's work can be found in *Union Spring Literary Review*, *Pleiades*, and *Voicemail Poems*, among others. Their debut collection, *Mythweaver*, will be published by *new words {press}* in summer 2025. You can learn more about them at linktr.ee/birchwiley.

⁎ **Cameron L. Mitchell** is a queer writer who grew up in the mountains of North Carolina. His work has appeared in *Vol. 1 Brooklyn*, *The Queer South Anthology*, *Literary Orphans*, *Gravel Literary Magazine*, and a few other places. He lives in New York and works in archives at Columbia University. Find him on Bluesky: @cameronlmitchell.bsky.social

⁎ **Casper Orr** (he/him) is a trans disabled writer and artist radically accepting his residence in New Jersey. He's a Senior Editor and Nonfiction Section Editor for *Fruitslice* while he studies literature and creative writing. He has previously contributed to *Fruitslice, Noise*

Made By, dadakuku, Transfix Magazine, The Bitchin' Kitsch, and more. Instagram and SubStack: @androqurrr

✳ **Charles K. Carter** (they/he) is a queer poet who lives in Oregon. They are the author of *The God of Loneliness* (Rebel Satori Press), *If the World Were a Quilt* (Kelsay Books), and *Read My Lips* (David Robert Books) as well as several chapbooks. Carter can be found on Instagram @CKCpoetry.

✳ **Christen Lee** is a family nurse practitioner in Cleveland, Ohio. Her writing has been featured in *Dulcet Lit, Rue Scribe, The Write Launch, Aurora, Humans of the World, Sad Girls Club, Encephalon, In Parentheses, The Elevation Review*, and *Moot Point* among others. Instagram @christen_a_lee_poet

✳ **Colleen S. Harris** (she/her) earned her MFA in Writing from Spalding University. A three-time Pushcart Prize nominee, her poetry collections include *The Light Becomes Us* (Main Street Rag, 2025), *Babylon Songs* (First Bite Press, forthcoming), *These Terrible Sacraments* (Bellowing Ark, 2010; Doubleback, 2019), *The Kentucky Vein* (Punkin House, 2011), *God in My Throat: The Lilith Poems* (Bellowing Ark, 2009), and chapbooks *That Reckless Sound* and *Some Assembly Required* (Pork Belly Press, 2014).

✳ **Eamon Dunn** (he/him) is a poet and essayist based in Chicago, IL. He attended the University of Vermont, where he earned a degree in English and won the Benjamin Wainwright Award for best poem, the Marion Berry Albee Award for excellence in composition, and the Daniel McCarter Award for LGBT studies. His work has been published in *The Gist, The Queen's Review, Raging Opossum Press*, and more. A 2025 Best of the Net nominee for poetry,

✳ **Ed Brickell** lives in Dallas, Texas. His poems have most recently been published in *The Harvard Advocate, Delta Poetry Review, Susurrus, Willawaw Journal*, and others. He just completed his first chapbook manuscript, *Wild Copenhagen*.

✳ **Elle Jay Snyder** (she/her) is a trans woman, poet, and part-time phantom from Staten Island. There was a longer version in which she sells herself. But she's tired, and possibly a little bloated...but like in a poetic way? Instagram: @ourladyofpoetics

✳ **Eric Best** mostly earned his living as a corporate consultant (Global Business Network 1990-95, Morgan Stanley 1996-2007) after an earlier life as a journalist 1971-89 (Lowell Sun, Stockton California Record, San Francisco Examiner, USA Today and 1983 Nieman Fellow.) He is the author of *Into My Father's Wake* (https://a.co/d/dTp9p90) about solo ocean sailing and growing up in New England (www.ericbestwriter.com), and a children's book, *The Deep*.

✳ **Erica Leslie Weidner** (she/they) is based, in New Jersey, and based in New Jersey. She is the founder and editor-in-chief of *underscore_magazine*. Wher she's not writing, she's at her day job doing badass librarian stuff.

✳ **ethan Viets vanlear** (he/him) is a black abolitionist poet born and raised on the far north side of Chicago. He is also the co-founder of Stick Talk, a mutual aid association co-created by young Black and Brown people who are both authors and survivors of gun-related harms, and the author of *Antidote*, his first completed collection of poetry. He is currently working on his second selection of poetry 'Code Switch'

✷ **George Oliver** (he/him) is a writer and researcher based in London, UK. He has a PhD in contemporary transatlantic literature and is the author of *Hybrid Novels: Post-postmodernism, Sincerity, and Race at the Turn of the 21st Century* (Routledge, forthcoming). His short stories have recently appeared or are forthcoming in Freshwater Literary Journal, grist, *The Interpreter's House*, and *Reverie,* and he was shortlisted for Ouen Press' 2019 Short Story Competition.

✷ **Grady VanWright** has been writing and reading poetry for personal enjoyment for over 25 years. Based in Houston, Texas, Grady draws inspiration from a lifetime of experiences, weaving together thoughtful reflections on life's complexities. His work often explores themes of introspection, independence, and the human condition.

✷ **Gray Dawson** (He/Him) is a Chicago born, openly queer individual who's main focus in writing is on growth in hardships and the resilence of the human spirit. He is currently attempting to get his degree in Creative Writing at Knox College and spends a majority of his time attempting to live life as fully as he can so he'll have more material.

✷ **Harry Edgar Palacio** (Hari) is a U.S born celebrity: numerous award-winning musician, author and fine artist. He hit #1 in Luxembourg & performed with Grammy winners and Grammy nominated artists including Ari Up, lead singer of The Slits 'Godmothers of Punk' former members of The Raincoats.

✷ **Helen Peluso** (she/her) is an MFA student in Fiction at Old Dominion University, in Norfolk, Virginia where her work won the annual Jerry Dickseski Fiction Prize and The American Academy of Poets' College Poetry Prize. Her work has been featured in *Constellate: A Student Anthology* and served as Florida Atlantic University's 2022-23 Student Writer in Residence. Her specialty is in literary fiction, with a specific focus on queer and feminist stories.

✷ **Holly Archibald** (she/her) is a working-class lesbian actor and poet based in Glasgow, Scotland. Her written work primarily focuses on lesbian identity, feminism, working-class culture, and open spirituality. Holly has most recently been published by Cerasus Magazine.

✷ **Jaweerya Mohammad** is a passionate educator whose writing is shaped by her Muslim and first-generation Pakistani American identity. Some of her poems have been published in the "Third Space" Anthology by *Renard Press* and *The Write Launch.* She has more writing forthcoming in *Qafiyah Review.* She firmly believes in the power of words, and that story-telling can foster a more empathetic and just world. You can find more of Jaweerya's work on Instagram (@jaweeryajournals)

✷ **Jennifer Anne Gordon** (she/they) is an award-winning horror author (Kindle Award Best Horror Novel 2020, Best Novel - Reader's Choice 2022, Lit Nastie Best Short Story of 2023, and Finalist for the Best Collection 2024-Chanticleer International Book Awards. Her CNF work has been featured in *Tangled Locks, Miniskirt Magazine,* and *The Nerd Daily.* She is a professional ballroom dancer, podcaster (Vox Vomitus) and queer burlesque performer living in a haunted house in New Hampshire.

✷ **Jess Tower** (she/they) is a disabled poet and educator from Danvers, Massachusetts. They live with their dog, Romeo, and their cat, Cole. Their partner, Teddy, is their most frequent visitor. Besides writing, Jess is also passionate about human rights and works with homeless people with local mutual aid groups. Jess has been published in

Soundings East, Meat for Tea: The Valley Review, Juked, A Thin Slice of Anxiety, and Tupelo Press's 30/30 project, among others.

✴ **Jiho Lee** is a writer, video game developer, and artist. Her novel, *Teddy Bears Under a Trash Compactor: Stories,* blends magical realism with a stream-of-consciousness narrative to depict alienation and the desire for human connection in the modern world. You can view more of her creative work at https://ujumiru.wixsite.com/jiholee.

✴ **Juheon Rhee** (she/her) is an 19-year-old South Korean writer residing in Waterloo. Her work has been published or is forthcoming in *Indolent Books, 580 Sprit, Lunch Ticket,* and *Cleaver Magazine* among others. She has also received nominations for her works, such as the Best of the Net Nomination.

✴ **Kali Joy Cramer** (he/she) is from the Chicago suburbs. He won a 2024 Ireland Chair of Poetry Student Award while completing an M.A. in Poetry at Queen's University Belfast. She is published in *Relief, The Broken Spine*, and *Metachrosis*, among others.

✴ **KD Hack** (they/he) is a Queer & Trans writer, baker, community tender, Death-Doula-In-Training & aspiring land steward. Their artistic practices were born & nourished across the Northwoods of Wisconsin, & currently live in the spaces between fingers in the soil & pencils on the page. Their work can be found in *Tence, Volume One, Hope is the Thing: Wisconsinites on Perseverance in a Pandemic, Barstow & Grand, & Better Homes & Dykes*, among others, as well as on his Substack, @joyfulcrumbs.

✴ **Kimberly Madura** is a social worker, traveler, essayist, and poet. She is originally from Indiana, and currently writes from a cabin in the woods of Vermont.

✴ **LE Francis** (she/her) is a recovering arts journalist writing poetry & fiction of varying length from the rainshadow of the Washington Cascades. Find her online at nocturnical.com.

✴ **Liz Yarwood** writes speculative fiction and poetry and is based in Berlin. She's interested in the pull of oblivion in its myriad forms, and nurtures an ever-growing fascination with the deep sea.

✴ **Lydia Rae Bush** is a poet exploring themes of embodiment and social-emotional development. Rae's work is Best of the Net nominated and appears in publications such as *Vocivia Magazine, Corporeal, and Sage Cigarettes Magazine*. When not writing, Lydia can be found singing and dancing, especially in bed when she is supposed to be going to sleep. Her chapbook "Free Bleeding" is out now with *dogleech books*.

✴ **Madari Pendas** is a Cuban-American writer, poet, painter, and cartoonist. She received her MFA from Florida International University, where she was a Lawrence Sanders Fellow, and won the 2021 Academy of American Poets Prize, judged by Major Jackson. Her work has appeared in *Craft, Smokelong Quarterly, The Masters Review, Oyster River Pages, PANK*, and more. She is the author of *Crossing the Hyphen* (2021) and *She Loves me, She Loves me Not* (2025), a queer love story told in poems.

✴ **Maggie Bowyer** (they/them) is a poet, cat parent, and the author of various poetry collections including *Homecoming* (2023) and *When I Bleed* (2021). Maggie has published work in *Chapter House Journal, Mantis, The B'K, The South Dakota Review, Querencia Press,* and more. They were the Editor-in-Chief of *The Lariat Newspaper*, a quarter-finalist at *Brave New Voices,* and a Marilyn Miller Poet Laureate. You can find their work on Instagram @maggie.writes.

✳ **Mateo Perez Lara** (they/them/theirs) is a queer, non-binary, Latinx poet from California. They have a pamphlet of poems, *Glitter Gods*, showcased with *Thirty West Publishing House*. They have an MFA in Poetry from Randolph College.

✳ **Maya Friedman** is a writer and artist living in Portland, Oregon. They write short fiction and lyric essays exploring queerness, dreams, bodies, and aesthetics.

✳ **Megan McCormack's** writing can be found in a variety of publications, like *Oyster River Pages* and Thimble. She earned her MFA in Fiction from the University of Missouri—St. Louis. Megan is a lower elementary Montessori teacher in Washington.

✳ **Mukund Gnanadesikan** (he/him) is the author of the 2020 novel Errors of Omission, the 2023 poetry chapbook Petit Morts: Meditations on Love and Death, and the 2023 children's picture book "Clarence and Elroy". His current projects include a full poetry collection arranged in the manner of a symphony, and a coming of age novel about adoption and addiction. When not writing, he practices medicine in California.

✳ **Naomi Simone Borwein** (she/her) is a Pushcart-nominated poet/academic. Some creative work appears or is forthcoming in *Utopia Science Fiction Magazine, Space & Time Magazine, HWA Poetry Showcase IX* (featured poet), *Lovecraftiana* (Candlemas and Walpurgisnacht), *Suburban Witchcraft Magazine, Rough Diamond Poetry, Ghost City Review, Zin Daily Literary*, and elsewhere. Naomi is also an editor in various guises.

✳ **Priya Saxena** (she/her) is a zine-maker and emerging poet based in Manhattan. She enjoys working on creative projects inspired by pop culture and her silly little lesbo life. Find her online on Twitter and Bluesky @lettersofpriya.

✳ **Rainier McCall** (he/they) is a Florida native, autistic abolitionist, Mad Pride advocate, survivor, cryptid, trauma therapist, and forever poet. Rainier is a contributor to many anthologies for survivors and abolitionists. Rainier is an agender trans person living with Ehlers Danlos type 1, POTS, and autism. Rainier can often be found verbally stimming to trap metal or dad rock, curating odds and ends from the Y2K period, and reading esoteric deep Florida literature.

✳ **Sarah Klein** is a genderfluid author currently residing in the greater Boston area. Their poems have previously been published *in fifth wheel press, Lammergeier, en*gendered, Olney Magazine's* "Reformatting the Pain Scale", and several others. They also enjoy voracious reading, baking, and being the change they want to see in the world. *Maddening Mast Cell Mathematics* is their first chapbook.

✳ **Sonya Wohletz** (she/her) is a writer whose work brings together image, history, and landscapes. Her work has appeared in Latin American Literary Review, Revolute, Roanoke Review, and others. Her first collection of poetry, *One Row After/Bir Sira Sonra*, was published by First Matter Press in 2022. She is a Pushcart Prize nominee.

✳ **Stacey Manos** (she/her/ella), 25, is a poet, playwright, and performance scholar based in New York City. Her original plays have been featured in collaboration with Breath of Fire Latina Theatre Ensemble, and New York Theatre Festival. She is an 11x published poet with work featured in *Poets Choice, Queer Rain,* and *Querencia Press*, among others. Her writing focuses on identity, grief, religion, and survival of sexual violence. You can access more of her writing at @skmpoetry on Instagram.

✳ **Tara Giancaspro** is the creator of xoxo Gossip Giancaspro, a weekly Substack (taragiancaspro.substack.com) including personal essays, pop culture commentary, and the various and sundry of her silly little life. She has been published in *Bullshit Lit, Wig-Wag Mag, Drunk Monkeys, Meow Meow Pow Pow Lit, Dusk Magazine*, and got bit by a dolphin once, establishing a potentially generational blood feud. Giancaspro can be found on Instagram and Twitter at @SweatyLamarr. She is based in New Jersey.

✳ **Tiezst "Tie" Taylor** is a Disabled, Black, and non-binary trans radical educator, artist-activist, poet, and storyteller. They have earned degrees in education and are a proponent of disability justice and abolitionist frameworks. Their work explores their experiences in surviving: Disability and severe mental illness and intersecting forms of oppression in the U.S. Tiezst was a Spring 2024 Brooklyn Poets Fellow and a past awardee of the NYSCA/NYFA Artists with Disabilities Grant.

✳ **Toma Zbrizher** (she/her) is a Ukrainian American poet. Her work has been published in various journals and anthologies. Her first full-length collection, *Tell Me Something Good*, was released from *Get Fresh Books* in 2019. She is the co-founder of *Yes&:NJ Creates*, an organization that offers free resources to NJ writers. She lives, writes, mothers and pets cats in the woods of New Jersey.

✳ **tommy wyatt** (he/they) is the jester of popular culture and poet laureate of timefuckery, who's synthesizing digital archives, space voids, and confines of the body. he's the author of *DITCHLAPSE / [REALLY AFRAID]; NOW THAT'S WHAT I CALL HORROR!; So, Who's Courage?; Trick Mirror or Your Computer Screen; disasterfire/disasterstar;* and others.

✳ **Xochitl-Julisa Bermejo** is the daughter of Mexican immigrants and author of *Incantation: Love Poems for Battle Sites* (Mouthfeel Press) and *Posada: Offerings of Witness and Refuge* (Sundress Publications). A former Steinbeck Fellow and Poets & Writers California Writers Exchange winner, Bermejo's writing can be found at *Acentos Review, Huizache, LA Review of Books,* and other journals. She teaches creative writing with Antioch University and is the director of Women Who Submit.